LIFE UNDERWATER

Matthew J. Metzger

A NineStar Press Publication

Published by NineStar Press
P.O. Box 91792,
Albuquerque, New Mexico, 87199 USA.
www.ninestarpress.com

Life Underwater

Printed in the USA
First Edition
October, 2018

Print ISBN: 978-1-949909-06-7

Also available in eBook, ISBN: 978-1-949909-02-9

Warning: This book contains hydrophobia, drowning, hints of familial transphobia and racism, and brief scenes of child endangerment.

Ashraf never thought he could fall in love. So when he falls hard and fast for marine biologist Jamie Singer, it's a shock to the system—in more ways than one.

Even if he can wrap his head around what love is and how relationships work, Ashraf's not sure this is viable. He's hydrophobic. And Jamie's entire world revolves around the sea. What's the point of trying if so much of Jamie's life is inaccessible to Ashraf?

But Ashraf has vastly underestimated the pull of loving Jamie. For the first time, he wants to face the water, rather than flee from it. He has underestimated the power of love in making people brave, stupid, or a little bit of both.

Maybe it's time to take a leap—and sink or swim.

Thanks to Omar and Shakil, for their feedback,
corrections, and semi-regular insults. I couldn't have done
it without you guys.

Chapter One

HE WAS GETTING funny looks.

It was an airport. Of course he was. It didn't matter that he was waiting at the arrivals gate, and he didn't have a bag. Ashraf *always* got funny looks in airports.

For once, though, he didn't care.

Because the flight from Sydney had clicked over to "arrived" nearly forty-five minutes ago. And Australian accents were starting to float out of the tunnel. His phone had already beeped in his pocket twice.

Jamie: *Landed safe, see you soon, love you! xxx*

Followed, not ten minutes later, by a second.

Jamie: *Don't go to mosque tonight? I want you all to myself. Please? xxx*

Six weeks was almost over.

Mosque could definitely wait.

He saw Professor Hanley first, with his customary battered backpack and fresh-from-the-jungle look. The man was a walking biohazard, and ticked every one of the absent-minded professor stereotypes, from the shabby jacket with the patched elbows to the Einstein-after-electrocution haircut. At his elbow loped his research assistant, George, looking like he'd not slept for the whole trip. He probably hadn't. And behind them, weighed down with souvenirs and suntans, their brand new PhD students, Meg and Jamie.

Ashraf began to smile.

The sight of Jamie, even after six weeks, was as familiar as though it had been six hours. That fluffy beanie hat. The strays of light-brown hair escaping around the edges. The spray of freckles that had eluded the sun cream. The small ears and sharp jaw, where Ashraf liked to trail his fingers down from shell to shoulder and feel the life underneath his touch. The bright, brilliant brown eyes that would dim shyly when he did.

That lit up like fireworks in the dark when their gazes met.

"Ashraf!"

The yell was like coming home. Warm. Wanted. Safe—even if the weight that smashed into his chest was anything but. Ashraf staggered, squeezing tight around skinny shoulders and trying to breathe past the scarf that smothered his face. Legs snaked around his thighs and clung too. He hadn't had a four-limbed hug in six weeks, and he never wanted to put them down.

But he did.

If only to catch both arms around a lean back, and kiss them.

Fists clutched at the front of his jacket. That beautiful face turned up into his own. Feet pushed up into perfect ballet points, and Ashraf could have stayed right there, holding his entire world in the circle of his arms, holding that weight like it was nothing, forever.

Even if he wasn't allowed.

The kiss was broken by a laugh, a nose rubbing against his own, and the brightest eyes in the world.

"Welcome home, Jamie."

"*Missed* you," Jamie enthused and wriggled against his chest as though hugging, without actually putting their arms around him. "What are you doing here? I was all set to surprise you at work!"

"I win," Ashraf said simply and squeezed. Jamie squeaked, coming up off their feet entirely. "I borrowed Tariq's car."

"Oh my God!"

"So do you need to go back with the others, or..."

"Or," Jamie said firmly and bounced up on the balls of their feet again to deliver a short, sharp kiss. "Let me just say goodbye. Stay right there. *Right* there!"

Ashraf obeyed. He couldn't stop smiling. He was getting funny looks again, but for an entirely different reason. Six weeks had been hard—but harder than he'd realised when Jamie smiled like that. Missing them had turned into a sharp, awful pain just with that one smile, and Ashraf didn't even like the ten feet that parted them as Jamie ricocheted around the others, collecting hugs from Meg and the professor, and pompously shaking George's hand before dragging him into a hug too.

So when they came back, still wearing their entire personality on their face, Ashraf reeled them in by the jacket and locked his arms around the small of their back.

"Hello," Jamie whispered against his mouth.

Ashraf silenced them, but only briefly before the laugh spoiled it, and Jamie was nuzzling his cheek.

"You've not shaved."

So?

"I like the bearded look. Very professorial."

Good.

"Bet Tariq doesn't know you borrowed the car to pick me up."

Nope.

"Bet he'd be pretty upset to get sin all over it too."

Probably.

"Want to get sin all over it?"

"Yes."

A smile creased against his cheek, and teeth gnawed lightly on his jaw before the warmth, the weight, the wonder, pulled away. The loss was staggering. Painful. Too soon.

"Come on," Jamie said. "Take me home in style."

Ashraf slid their fingers together and decided to take the scenic route.

IT WAS A long drive home. But Tariq's car was a soft-top, and the sun was out. And Tariq had a hundred speeding fines and didn't care—or pay them—so Ashraf put his foot down, and England rushed past in a blur of concrete barriers, roadworks, and dusty trees. Jamie was all enthusiasm to Northampton and then fell asleep with their scarf over their head and shoulders like a hijab. Ashraf pulled in at the services to put the roof back up and took the rest of the journey in quiet peace.

He'd only been with Jamie since this past May, but it still surprised him how it all felt. Ashraf wasn't really one for relationships. Had always thought he'd turn into one of those old professors with a collection of dusty old books, a huffy Persian cat, and a thing for cognac. Given he didn't drink, he wasn't sure how he was going to develop the thing for cognac, but that had been the destination.

Then Jamie had kissed him at that bus stop.

They'd been—not friends, exactly, but on nodding terms for a long time. They'd both been regulars attending the university debate club, and Ashraf hadn't even known their name. Then one evening, they got to talking after a particularly interesting motion, and Jamie asked Ashraf to walk them to the bus stop as it was after dark.

Then they'd kissed him and breathlessly asked him out.

Ashraf had sunk, right then and there.

It had been a strange experience. The whole street had vanished around him. The only thing he could see was Jamie's eyes, and he'd noticed every detail about them. The tiny threads of black that streaked through the deep brown, subtle and understated. The way their eyelashes curved. The freckle under their left eye, maybe on their nose and maybe just shy of it. The way their gaze roamed the middle-distance, looking at some invisible six-foot-tall object when they stammered out the question.

And his own heartbeat, thundering in his chest. His own breathing, raking through his throat.

He'd never fallen in love before, but Ashraf was fairly certain that had been what it was. The feeling, the cause.

Once, he'd have laughed at the idea of driving from Newcastle to London in a friend's car to pick someone up from the airport. Let them get another flight. Let them get a train. But he'd wanted to surprise Jamie, and get another one of those beautiful smiles. And even though the company was crap, being fast asleep and boring for a little while, he didn't regret a minute of it.

Jamie performed the passenger trick of waking up ten minutes from their destination. They woke up quickly, stretching and smacking their elbows off the roof before giving him a dirty look.

"You closed it," they said accusingly.

"You'd have lost your scarf."

"Eh. I have other scarves."

"You'd have complained," Ashraf said flatly, and Jamie laughed.

"And you would have pulled a face, ignored me, and bought me another one."

"Maybe not."

"You did last time. Hey. Why are we going this way?"

"Uh, because that's the way to the flat?"

Jamie stuck out their lower lip. "I don't want to go to the flat."

"Eh?"

"Shane will be in."

Ashraf racked his brain. "You have a row or something?"

"No, dipshit. I like Shane fine, but I'm not up for a third wheel right now, get it? Your house. Go."

Ashraf flicked the indicator and changed lanes with a laugh.

"I thought you'd want to drop off your gear and shower."

"I can do that at your house."

"Want to stay the night?"

"*God* yes."

Ashraf smiled as he joined the main road crawling towards the coast. He'd never driven out that far, but it seemed like everyone and their mother wanted to today.

"Make you a deal," he said.

"Hm?"

"If you let me hug you for a bit, I'll spring for whatever dinner you want."

"What*ever* dinner I want?"

"Yeah."

"Even if it's homemade?"

Ashraf pretended to think about it. "Hmm...yeah, okay."

"Deal," Jamie said immediately and wriggled down in the seat to put their boots on the dash. "Drive, motherfucker. You got a sex bomb to get to bed."

Ashraf laughed...and nudged the accelerator down just a fraction further.

ASHRAF DOZED.

Jamie was the active sort—always swimming, always dancing, always on the move—but it was moments like this that Ashraf loved the most. When the world slowed down and stilled, and he could drift grounded only by the smooth, soft skin searing hot against his own. The tickle of hair at his neck. The gentle brush of every breath over his chest. The sensuality of having a bare breast pressed against his arm, and the delicate trust of the toes tucked between his knees.

Perfection.

And disturbed by a rumble of thunder outside. The sound washed over them both and broke the peace like ripples on a still koi pond. Jamie stirred. Ashraf caught at the knee bent over his belly and stroked the smooth cap before it was tugged away. A kiss warped by a wide smile landed on his mouth.

"Feed me," Jamie implored, and Ashraf sighed.

"All right, all right..."

He left Jamie naked in the tangled sheets and padded equally naked out down the stairs into the main room. The house was tiny, little more than one studio flat placed on top of another, a spiral staircase joining them. The ground floor was a single room, a kitchenette crammed into a messy living room brimming over with books. The first floor was almost all bedroom, with windows on both sides, and a tiny bathroom no bigger than that of an aeroplane squeezed into a spare corner. All the furniture was old, and none of the décor matched. Ashraf's prayer mat was a splash of colour over the back of the brown leather sofa, and the stairs were decorated with drying laundry. Outside, it was just as squashed. The front opened straight onto the pavement, and there was no back garden at all. And it was in the middle of a narrow street of terraced houses, all crushed into the gap between a now-destroyed mill and the shell of a long-closed factory.

But Ashraf loved it.

It was *home*.

He found a couple of stray Chinese ready meals in the freezer, stabbed the cling film tops, and leaned against the counter with a book while they turned in the microwave. He got through a chapter on the substandard nature of the Russian arms supplied during the Spanish Civil War before the smell of chicken in black bean sauce began to permeate the air. And once the smell had leaked out—

Boards creaked overhead.

Ashraf smiled as he opened the little door and dumped the meals into one big bowl to share. By the time he'd fished forks out of the cutlery drawer, the TV had been switched on, and he turned to see Jamie stretched out on the sofa, wearing Ashraf's tartan pyjama bottoms and nothing else. They had—of course—already commandeered the remote.

They both ate in relative silence. It was a comfortable, familiar thing. Jamie was bleary-eyed with sleep, nodding off more than once against Ashraf's shoulder, and Ashraf turned the volume down on the TV and let them. When he'd put the empty bowl aside, he turned to slide his leg under Jamie's thighs and tipped them both down onto the cushions to cuddle.

Jamie sighed, draped an arm over Ashraf's waist, and squeezed.

"Missed you," they murmured, burying their face in Ashraf's neck.

Ashraf smiled and said nothing. Slowly, Jamie settled. They twisted onto their side, jammed under Ashraf's arm and into the impossibly small gap between him and the back of the sofa, and dozed with their leg slung over both of Ashraf's in an oddly possessive gesture. Their head dropped slowly until Ashraf could press his nose to a warm, delicate crown, and inhale a familiar, long-lost scent.

His heart *ached.*

"Love you," he whispered, and the arm about his waist squeezed again.

Ashraf folded up a hand to stroke a single finger down bare ribs. He felt soft skin. The gentle pucker of a scar that couldn't even be seen. The graceful swell of a small breast. When he stroked the nipple with the back of his nail, the responding hum was heavy and peaceful. Pure bliss swept over him, like sinking into a hot bath.

It was like being allowed to breathe, for the first time in six weeks.

When had it come to this? When had cinema dates and Italian lessons over German meatballs turned into something so perfectly wonderful? When he had fallen, *really* fallen, in love?

"Jamie."

"Mm?"

"Would you—?"

He touched the back of his nail to that nipple again. Felt the weight of a thigh over his hips. Saw, at the very end of the sofa, the abandoned beanie hat. And between himself and the hat, his stolen pyjama bottoms.

"What?"

"Move in with me."

Chapter Two

ASHRAF WAS AWAKE before the first light of dawn.

He always was—Fajr and breakfast weren't things he liked to combine—but usually when he was done, he would put the prayer mat away and start to get ready for work. It meant he always got in early, and could usually leave early. It was a good deal.

That morning, though, he sat back on his heels and stared at the bed.

Jamie was normally a light sleeper, but they were clearly still jet-lagged. They had turned over into the warm spot Ashraf had left behind, and their face was almost completely buried in his pillow. It was a marvel they hadn't suffocated. Their hair was a bird's nest, their naked legs still marked by twenty-four hours of airline compression socks, and the serene divinity of their bare form, as beautiful as Allah could make any living being, was disturbed by the strangled snore.

Ashraf smiled and shuffled forward on his knees to grasp a bare ankle and kiss the scuffed heel of a much-loved foot.

He was still getting used to this. Having someone else in his space, and actually enjoying it. His lack of relationships was something he'd never missed before. In truth, he would have been perfectly happy to live out his days without them. But now he *had* Jamie, it would hurt like hell to let them go. It was an adjustment he wasn't entirely done with making.

Did other people sense their partner's presence as Ashraf did? Jamie stayed resolutely asleep as Ashraf showered again, trimmed his beard, put a load of laundry in, ate—but he could almost feel them in the house, like a peaceful ghost. He had company, even though he was entirely alone.

And it fell away when he stepped outside and closed the front door behind him. He set off to work with a smile.

Ashraf worked at the university. It had been a return, of sorts—he'd done his PhD at Newcastle, but his first research post had been at York and the second at Liverpool. He'd been gone five years before the lecturer's position came up, and he applied more out of hopeful nostalgia than anything else. He returned to the Toon to find it hadn't really changed—to a nice office and plenty of time for his research, and a small teaching responsibility of a couple of modules on Roman archaeology. It wasn't even his specialism, but Ashraf was an Italian history graduate with an interest in ancient history and anthropology. Of course, the Romans had been part of it.

He liked his job, and he liked Newcastle. It had been a struggle for a long time—the accent was horrific, never mind the impenetrable dialect—but the people were friendly and had been patient with him. It was easy to stay in the safe cocoon of the city centre and the university buildings. It had a river, but he didn't need to see it; it had a beach, but it was easily avoided. He'd made a handful of friends, and the students seemed to enjoy his seminars. The head of the department liked him and his work and had promised that after a couple of years, Ashraf would almost certainly get a proper professorial post. He'd found a nice house, returned to a welcoming mosque, and—though he'd never looked for one—found a partner. The future was good, and this was home now.

And getting better, judging by the beauty in his bed that morning.

Ashraf cycled into work. It was cool and sunny. A wind was blowing in from the unseen sea, more refreshing than any cup of coffee. Not that it stopped him from getting said cup, after locking his bike to the railings at the front of the building. The order was memorised by heart: two tall mochas and a skinny cappuccino with extra sprinkles. He juggled them expertly as he shouldered his way through several doors, hiked up two flights of stairs, and shuffled backwards through a door marked with a still-strange sign.

Dr Layton, Dr Blake, Dr Zaccaria.

"Thank God!"

Ashraf smirked and delivered a mocha into Kath's grasping hands.

"And good morning to you too."

"In a minute," she said, eyes blissfully closed over the steaming cardboard cup. "This is why you're my favourite. Time to step up, Tom!"

Tom rolled his eyes, offered a vague thanks for the cappuccino, and disappeared back into a vast tome of crispy, fragile pages that he was turning with gloved hands.

"Should that really be in here?" Ashraf asked doubtfully.

"It's fine," Tom murmured, almost to himself.

"Church records," Kath supplied, and Ashraf immediately lost interest. Tom was studying prehistoric religion. Ashraf was just as convinced as he was that Stone Age man had had religion—they'd had art, hunting strategy, and tribal warfare, so why not religion?—but Ashraf had no interest in it. And Tom was a bear in the midst of a discovery, so Ashraf quietly tucked his bag under his desk, sifted through his piles of notes for the keyboard, and struggled to remember his password. He had a handful of emails from his former first-years, mostly asking after references. One enterprising soul wanted suggestions on their final year thesis already; Ashraf flagged it for later and kept going. A conference invite. Couple of generic submissions calls for journals. Ashraf eyed one and flagged it for his work with Dr Martinez on the ancient cultural exchange between the Iberian peninsula and North Africa.

Then Tom closed the tome, slid it into a plastic bag, and emerged from his academic stupor.

"Good weekend?"

Ashraf grinned at his monitor. "Yep."

"Oh, there's a story," Kath cackled. "Go out and get some, did you?"

The smile dimmed a fraction. "Nope."

"Eid?" Tom guessed.

"That was ages ago."

"Recovered from Eid indigestion?" Kath suggested. "That takes ages too."

Ashraf laughed but shook his head.

"Oh!" Tom snapped his fingers. "Jamie was due back yesterday, wasn't she?"

"They. And yes."

"Shit, they, sorry." Tom grimaced and then grinned. "Surprised you're even in, then. You must have been shagging like rabbits."

Ashraf rolled his eyes. "Nope."

"Jet lag," Tom declared confidently. "You'll go home early and come in walking funny tomorrow."

"What you do with your partners is entirely up to you," Ashraf said loftily.

"Knock it off, Tom." Kath's voice was a little sharp.

"All right, all right. So, celebrating their homecoming?"

"And the rest," Ashraf said, allowing the megawatt grin to take over his face again. "I asked them to move in with me yesterday—"

"Holy hell!"

"—and they said yes."

Actually, Jamie had squealed as if Ashraf had proposed. But the word yes had been in there, several times, so it wasn't a lie.

"Christ," Tom said. "You'll be getting sodding married next. Well. Congratulations!"

"I don't know about that," Ashraf said doubtfully. "I've never cohabited before."

"Cohabited," Tom mimicked. "Shacked up with."

"Whatever."

"And really? Never?"

"Not with a partner."

"Huh. Well. Good luck."

"Thanks?"

"You'll need it." Tom chuckled as he began to gather his things off the desk. "Wait until you get snoring in your ear and cold feet on your balls every day. Then you'll be singing a different tune."

"Yeah, yeah. Oh, drop this into the library collection bin for me?"

"Git. If Dr Collins comes looking for me, I'll be going down to the county archives after dropping this lot off."

He slammed his way out, a typical Tom-shaped tornado, and Ashraf sighed, looking at a quiet Kath. She was typing in a very slow, deliberate manner, and avoiding his gaze.

"Go on then."

She blinked over the top of her monitor. "Go on what?"

"Say it. I know you want to."

She pursed her lips. Then said, "Is living with Jamie really a good idea?"

Her voice was cool and very collected. Stitched together, almost, so no inflection could be misinterpreted. It was diplomatic, but Ashraf found himself grinding his teeth a little anyway. They'd had the argument before. Plenty of times.

But he tried to be just as even. "I asked, they agreed. We both think it's time to try it."

"She's only twenty-three."

"Which is a whole seven years older than sixteen," Ashraf replied, maybe a little too sarcastically.

"She's a *student*."

Ashraf clenched his jaw a little. His typing paused.

"They. And I'm aware of that."

"I just—I can't get my head around it, Ashraf." Her tone had turned a little pleading. Ashraf had to set his hands down on the edge of the desk to stop them from trembling. "She's—they're—a student. They're, what, fourteen years younger than you? Thirteen?"

"Twelve."

"And they're vulnerable. LGBT students are vulnerable."

She said it emphatically. Dogmatically. The departmental training had done its work.

"Look," Ashraf said tightly. "I understand your concern. But Jamie's not *my* student. They've not studied history since they were in school, and they've never studied anthropology at all. There's no power thing here, Kath."

She shook her head silently, and Ashraf gave up. He didn't want a blistering row again, and Kath had always hated this. She'd been horrified when he'd announced he had a date with a student. And he got it—kind of. If Jamie were in the same department, or some naïve eighteen-year-old freshman straight out of school, it would definitely feel a bit skeevy. But they weren't, so it didn't.

"We'll have to agree to disagree," came the crisp reply.

They agreed to disagree in total silence. Ashraf usually minded, but his jubilation at Jamie's ecstatic yes was carrying over, and he found himself pleasantly making plans instead of working. He'd have to get another set of shelves for all of Jamie's books. And they'd insisted the fish had to come with them, so a corner would have to be found for the aquarium. Ashraf hated any body of water bigger than a bath, but even he could tolerate the shoebox that was the fish tank. Perhaps it could go behind the stairs.

Kath left at half ten for a meeting without saying goodbye. Ashraf managed to clear out a few more emails before drifting back to drawing on a scrap of paper, rearranging his furniture to fit a fish tank and a forest of books. Tom came back just before lunch and suggested Ashraf just put the fish in the sink.

"Only fish, aren't they? Just add water."

"They're fancy tropical fish."

"What've they got fancy tropical fish for?"

Ashraf shrugged, reaching for his phone when it buzzed. "They do marine biology, they're not really supposed to have a cat, are they?"

Jamie: *Tariq's just turned up to...*

"Suppose so."

Ashraf hummed as he swiped open the text.

Jamie: *Tariq's just turned up to collect his car. I don't think he likes me. Got proper grumpy xxx*

Ashraf: *Sounds about right. Got any plans for the day?*

Jamie: *Got to pick up some stuff from admin. Meet you for lunch? If you're not busy, want to go to the beach and celebrate with some ice creams? The cafe on the front is proper 1950s, it's cute!! xxx*

Ashraf winced.

Ashraf: *Pass for today? Just fancy our usual tbh.*

Jamie: *Another time then :) Maybe next week. And why doesn't Tariq like me this time? Xxx*

More like next life.

Ashraf: *Usual place at 12? :) And same reasons as always.*

Jamie: *If I rub my white queer atheist hands all over your front door will he stop coming over? xxx*

Ashraf snorted with laughter.

Ashraf: *The atheism definitely isn't the issue.*

Jamie: *Everything else is though, right? xxx*

Ashraf: *Probably. But he doesn't know you're queer.*

Jamie: *I'M GOING TO PAINT YOUR DOOR RAINBOW!*

Ashraf: *Leave him alone. We won't get to borrow his car and get queer all over the back seat if you annoy him.*

It still felt a little odd, writing the word queer. It had been a slur when Ashraf was growing up, but things had moved on without him, it seemed. Jamie actively identified as such. Hard to say they were straight, they kept pointing out, if they weren't a woman. Ergo, queer. Ashraf didn't quite understand the logic, but then he'd never liked anyone before anyway.

Jamie: *Ooh, true. Best behaviour then! Leaving now. See you at 12ish! xxx*

Ashraf glanced up at the clock on the wall. It was quarter to already. Jamie would have to get the bus.

Ashraf: *Meet you there. Usual?*

Jamie: *Please! xxx*

"Want anything from Costa?"

"Nah, mate, I'm good."

The wind blowing in from the sea had gone cold when Ashraf headed out. He walked rather than took the bike, to give Jamie's bus a chance to deliver them, and enjoyed the fresh air. It had been a grim but still summer. Everyone had spent all their time on the seafront, but Ashraf refused to go anywhere near it, so he'd spent most of it shut away in various libraries and archives and getting some work done. Now that Jamie was back, maybe he could take a week off. They'd have to have a few days to get everything moved in and settled, right?

Jamie turned up just as Ashraf was ordering, bouncing into the queue with a toastie and adding it to Ashraf's tray with a beaming smile and a kiss on the cheek.

"Thought you could treat me!" they trilled, to the great amusement of the barista. Ashraf pulled a face but didn't argue, and slid an arm around their waist to hug them as they both waited. "Mm, hello. Miss me?"

"Yep."

Jamie drummed their fists lightly against Ashraf's chest and stretched up on their toes for another kiss. "Busy?"

"Not too bad. I could be not busy again."

"Be not busy again," Jamie said and rubbed their nose against Ashraf's. "I might have already sent my change of address form into the university."

Ashraf smiled. "Lunch then back to the house?"

"Via the shops, seeing as you won't come and get ice cream. Celebratory new fleece!"

"You and your fleeces," Ashraf complained, only for Jamie to laugh at him.

"You love me in my fleeces," came the tart reply—and then, right in his ear: "Especially me in *just* my fleeces."

Ashraf stroked a thumb dangerously over the slip of thin hip showing between jeans and jackets—and stepped away to collect their order. Jamie put on an impressive sulk all the way to their favourite table by the window, then sat back with a sunny smile and stuck their feet right between

Ashraf's under the table.

"I didn't drink a single cup of coffee all the time I was in Australia," they said, and Ashraf blinked.

"Really?"

"Mhmm. Felt too lonely without you."

"Did your fellow fish friends not help?"

"No." Jamie rolled their eyes. "It has to be lactose-free, sugar-free, fair trade, vegan-approved decaf if Meg's around."

"So, water?"

"Basically."

"I'm guessing your coffee machine is moving in too?"

"Of course," Jamie said loftily and set their cup down. "I wanted to ask, actually…"

"Oh, no. I'm not squeezing Tabitha onto the sofa too."

"I wasn't going to bring Tabitha!" came the laughing reply. "She'll be over all the time anyway. No, um…I wanted to ask if you had any plans for my birthday?"

"Uh…"

"It's not a trick question."

"Then, no."

"So…do you want to go somewhere with me?"

Yes. "Depends on where. And who else is there."

"Um. Well. If you want, just you and me."

Ashraf raised his eyebrows. It wasn't exactly a huge number—twenty-four wasn't especially significant—but Jamie was sociable at the best of times. "What about Tabby? And Shane?"

"Oh, we'll have a piss-up at some point. See—this PhD."

"What's that got to do with your birthday?"

"I'm *telling* you!"

"All right, all right!"

"I'm studying the methodology and viability of artificial

reefs."

"Come again?"

Jamie laughed. "The coral reefs are dying. So how do we best make new ones, and where?"

"Oh. How?"

"Oh, I have three years to figure that out, that'll be fine." Jamie waved a hand airily. "Anyway, there's already an artificial one off the coast of Jordan on the Red Sea. One of the royal family sunk a ship and a coral reef grew on it. And Professor Hanley has secured a little bursary for flights so we can go and take a look, as part of our research, around my birthday."

"You want to go to Jordan for your birthday?"

"Well, it's just before. And I have some savings and you have some savings and I thought maybe we could upgrade to a proper little resort and just...extend our trip a few days?"

"How long?"

"Whole thing—I was thinking about a week, maybe?"

A week on the Red Sea with Jamie for their birthday? Ashraf hadn't been to Jordan, but Mamma had been Egyptian, and he'd been there several times when he was a kid. All he could really remember was intense heat and an endless blue sky. A week with Jamie in a—whatever they wore to swim in hotel pools, in that weather?

He'd been saving up for a new bike, but...

"That'd be amazing," he said, and Jamie beamed at him over the table.

To hell with Kath's opinion. This was all going to be amazing.

Chapter Three

JAMIE WASN'T AROUND much that last week before the university term started. They shot off to visit their mum in Scotland, and Ashraf was left once more to his own devices. He didn't mind. It gave him time to shift the furniture around, and prepare.

He hadn't lived with a partner in...ever. There'd never really *been* a partner before Jamie. And it had been so long since he'd roomed with anyone—a decade, Ashraf realised with a shock—that he'd forgotten what sharing his space on a permanent basis was even like. There were going to be some adjustments to be made.

The week apart made Ashraf antsy, despite the nerves. He felt oddly addicted. He found himself stroking his bare hip and arm in bed, trying to imagine it was Jamie's skin and not his own. He went to mosque twice, just to avoid the empty house with the sofa in its new position. The space for the fish tank looked like a hole.

Now Jamie had agreed to move in with him, their absence felt *wrong.*

And then halfway through Ashraf's first lecture of the academic year, at half past two on Monday afternoon, his phone vibrated three times against his leg, and the jittery tension evaporated. Poof. Gone. Just like that.

Jamie was back.

When the last half hour of pointless introductions and course overviews was up, Ashraf checked his phone before he'd even closed his laptop. The message wasn't much—*Tom says you're boring some freshmen to death, when can I have you back?*—but it made him smile all the same.

Ashraf: *Now :)*

The reply was immediate.

Jamie: *Yes! Missed you, want a foot massage xxx*

Ashraf: *Oh, I get it. You missed my hands.*

Jamie: *Always :**

Ashraf: *Will pass Costa. Meet you there?*

Jamie: *Yes! Xxx*

He didn't amble this time. It was drizzling outside, and he turned his collar up, put his head down, and marched for their meeting point with determination. The trouble with universities was it was impossible to cross the campus without being stopped for a chat, and Ashraf had no intention of being delayed. He just wanted to go home. With Jamie.

The person in question was waiting outside with a steaming cup when Ashraf turned the corner onto the street. Beads of rainwater were glittering on the fluffy surface of their hat. They beamed and rocked up on their toes to deliver a coffee-dark kiss, and laughed when Ashraf caught at the back of their belt to help.

"Miss me too?"

"Yes. I have to drop off my gear in the office, but home after that?"

"Mine or yours?"

"Mine. Soon to be yours."

Jamie whistled, breaking free only to slide an arm through Ashraf's, tight, as though they were sharing an invisible brolly.

"How was Edinburgh?"

"Wet," they said. "Mam wasn't too impressed at my news."

Ashraf's stomach tightened. "Why?"

"Mostly because she's never met you, and Ellie's got just as shit a taste in men as Mam had. So we're not too good at boyfriends in my family."

"What about your other sister?"

"Gay."

"Ah." Ashraf tightened his arm to squeeze Jamie's hand to his side. "Yeah, well, your taste is much better."

"Infinitely," Jamie proclaimed proudly. "She'll like you fine when she meets you."

"When?"

"Yeah, I have to bring you up for the baby's christening."

Ashraf drew a blank. "What baby?"

"I told you! Ellie's baby!"

"I thought she had a four-year-old?"

"She does, and she's pregnant. She's due next month. Learn to listen! You're such a *man*."

Ashraf laughed and grabbed Jamie around the waist to roughly hoist them into the air and dump them off the pavement into a puddle.

"Oh my God, you *arse!*"

"Still think you have better taste in men?"

Jamie's outraged face softened, and they bounced up onto the kerb again to slide an arm around Ashraf's neck and nuzzle at his beard.

"In-fin-ite-ly," they said slowly—then pinched.

"Ow!"

"Learn to listen!"

Ashraf grumbled, sliding Jamie off to the side. "Yeah, yeah. Anyway, you can't go to a christening. Don't you burst into flames when you go into houses of worship?"

"I do a satanic ritual first to protect myself. And I wear non-flammable clothes," Jamie deadpanned.

"Might test that theory..."

"Cheeky shit," Jamie said as they reached the department building. They held the door and then obnoxiously slid a hand into Ashraf's back pocket once they were inside. "This is nice."

"Letch."

"And proud."

Ashraf retrieved the hand as they approached the office door, tapping the wrist sharply before letting go.

"I was thinking we could move your stuff in at the weekend," he said. "I moved everything around already."

"Could do it Wednesday night." Jamie shrugged. "You haven't got any lectures, and Shane's offered to help heft all the boxes."

Wednesday. Ashraf's fingers nearly slipped on the doorknob. They could be moved in by Wednesday.

"Okay," he said a little hoarsely. "Wednesday it is."

Then he popped open the office door—and locked eyes with Kath.

She'd obviously heard their voices in the corridor. Not only were her eyes narrowed at him, but she didn't look remotely surprised to see Jamie, despite the fact that Jamie rarely came up to the office.

"Hey, Kath," Jamie said absently, seemingly oblivious. They kicked Ashraf's shoe. "Come on! Get your stuff and let's go."

Ashraf grunted. His mood soured instantly at the look on Kath's face. Her lips were pursed. She looked more like someone's disapproving mother than his colleague.

"Everything all right, Jamie?" she asked.

Jamie blinked, turning from Ashraf's desk as he gathered his gear.

"Uh. Yeah. You?"

"Fine. Got plans?"

"Not much."

"C'mon." Ashraf slung his messenger bag over his shoulder, throwing Kath a dirty look. He knew he was probably making things worse, but her narrow-eyed suspicion was making the hairs on the back of his neck stand on end.

"What was that about?" Jamie asked once they were out of the building and Ashraf was unlocking his bike from the railing.

"What?"

"Kath. And you, actually. Have a row?"

Ashraf grimaced. "She's not comfortable with—us. You and me dating."

"Why?"

"Lecturer. Student."

Jamie snorted. "She'll get over it." They slid up onto the bike saddle with a smirk. "C'mon, then, *professor*. Push me."

Ashraf pulled a face—but started to push.

JAMIE DIDN'T WAIT until Wednesday.

Ashraf answered the doorbell on Tuesday morning to Tabitha's woolly hat and wide grin over a box of assorted belongings, and Shane's beat-up car parked right outside his front door. He and Jamie were gingerly lifting the fish tank—thankfully empty—out of the boot.

"Oh," Ashraf said.

"Come on, Raf, budge over!" Tabitha said cheerfully and elbowed right past him into his living room.

Jamie was one of those people who came with their friends. They and Shane—now a junior doctor—went back to their first year in halls together. They had a similar sense of humour, apparently, though Ashraf didn't think he'd ever heard Shane say more than a handful of words. Tabby had been an acquisition from the drama society and was in her final year of an engineering degree. She talked to—or rather at—Ashraf a lot more, but thankfully never seemed to expect much response.

It was a nice combination. While neither of Jamie's closest friends seemed to expect Ashraf to interact with them much—a blessing for someone as uninterested in people as him—it was still clear that Jamie wouldn't be parted from them. Ashraf had learned from the very first date that Jamie was a package deal. They were sweet and soulful with him—but with their friends, they were a firework.

"Ashraf!"

He laughed and caught the kiss aimed his way around the bulging bag of fish before stepping aside. A beautiful firework. He retreated to the kitchenette, to cups and teabags, and left them to it. Jamie was effusive and chatty, their noise bubbling around the little house as the three of them hefted in boxes and bags. Ashraf handed out the mugs as the flow of belongings slowed and eventually stopped, and took himself off upstairs to change the sheets on the bed as they argued over the best way to set up the tank.

Just after he got the last of the pillows done, the front door closed downstairs. Quiet. It washed through the house, but he could feel Jamie was still there and smiled as he made for the stairs. Was this what cohabiting was like? The ability to just feel if Jamie was in the house?

He could get used to that.

Ashraf walked slowly down the stairs. Jamie's things were piled in bags at the bottom of them. They hadn't brought pans or towels or linens—Ashraf had told them not to bother. Still, there was a reasonable pile of things. Their diving gear, for one. A sports bag overflowing with their clubbing outfits. Boxes upon boxes of books, and Ashraf had no doubt that was after a clean-out. A carefully packed crate containing their PC and laptop, both high spec and—any time Ashraf had ever seen them using it—brimming over with their research.

And in the living room, tucked under the stairs, Jamie. Looking like they had a hundred times before in Ashraf's house, with their bare feet and mussed hair, hands cupped around a mug of tea like it was cold. Only, somehow, they looked like they belonged more than ever before, peering into their fish tank and for once ignoring Ashraf's presence.

Like there was no time limit. Like there was no going home.

"Fish okay?"

"I think so." Jamie straightened up and edged sideways into Ashraf's reach to cosy up to his chest. "Hi."

They tipped their head winningly back on his shoulder. Ashraf rolled his eyes, ruffled their hair, and peered at the fish.

"I don't have to help with them, right?"

He'd never had fish. They were tiny. And weird colours. They flashed like nightclub signs.

"Only when I clean the tank. Then you just hold the bowl and do as you're told." Jamie nudged his elbow, grinning at the bundle of dirty sheets ready for the wash. "You planning something?"

"Yeah. Laundry."

Jamie pouted. Ashraf chuckled, breaking away to shove the sheets in the washing machine. When he turned back, Jamie had lost interest in flirting and was peering into the tank again. Key to Ashraf's plot, they'd put their mug of tea down.

"I didn't think fish really cared if you loved them or not."

"They don't; I just like watching them."

"Uh-huh." Ashraf looped his arms around Jamie's waist, hoisted them away from the tank, and brought them both crashing down onto the sofa. Jamie laughed and squirmed over until they were tangled up in a messy hug together, and Jamie's mouth was somewhere near Ashraf's ear.

"This is good," they mumbled.

Ashraf had to agree.

Chapter Four

IT FELT A little strange, going out to mosque and leaving the lights on.

Ashraf usually got a lift to Friday prayers, either from Tariq or the imam's wife. But that first Friday after Jamie moved in, Tariq was in Manchester probably doing something illegal, and Humaira texted him to say their little lad wasn't well so she'd be staying home. Part of Ashraf wanted to stay home and soak up the new atmosphere in the house, but...it was *Friday*.

"Go!" Jamie said eventually when they saw him dithering over his prayer mat. "I'm only going to type up my thesis notes anyway. We can be fluffy when you get back."

"Fluffy?" Ashraf objected mildly, but picked up the mat and folded it into its bag. "You sure?"

"You'll only feel crap if you miss Friday; you always do."

Ashraf grimaced.

"Go on." Jamie extended a bare foot from their spot on the sofa to prod his shin. "Shoo. Go pray, god-botherer."

"Heathen."

Jamie saluted with a grin, and Ashraf stooped to kiss them quickly.

"Okay. Be back by ten."

"Stay safe."

He shut the door on the quiet command and frowned. Stay safe. The one time—apart from Ramadan—when he felt truly ill at ease.

It was hard to be obviously Muslim these days. Too much hatred on the front pages of tabloid newspapers; too many extreme right wing types allowed to bleat their idiocy to anyone who'd listen. Racism and Islamophobia all wrapped up together. It had been an uncomfortable situation when Ashraf had first come to the UK, and it had only gotten worse since.

But Ashraf was lucky. For starters, he was a man. And most of the time, he didn't wear anything that revealed his faith, his scruffy jeans and close-cropped beard disguising his beliefs under a layer of generic neutrality. He didn't live in a Muslim area of the city, he didn't have friends and family nearby whose faith was more obvious than his own, and he didn't pray in public. He was Muslim enough to earn a sideways glance or two on a crowded bus, but western enough to ward off anything worse.

But on Fridays, he wore his jalabiya.

Some didn't. Plenty of the younger lads, especially, turned up in their everyday clothes. It would probably be safer to do that, on the days he had to get there on his own. But it was a hangover from his mother's family—mosque was formal. Mosque was proper. One didn't go to mosque in grubby jeans and Nike trainers any more than one would go to Sunday mass in them. And with a Christian father and a Muslim mother, Ashraf had dabbled in both religions before settling into the soft curves and warm tongue of the mosques. So when he went to pray, his clothing marked him out.

Thankfully, there was a direct bus that took him from a street away from his house to two streets away from the mosque. He'd learned to get the last possible one in order to arrive on time. By the time he stepped down off the bus, there were little old bangers stuffed with young families searching for a parking space, and elderly gents shuffling in pairs towards the low, rolling call that was beginning to drift from the minaret. There was safety in numbers. Security. The closer he got to the yellow light spilling from the open doors into the gloom, the more comfortable Ashraf felt.

And when he stepped inside, he felt Allah wrap around him like a shield.

He'd grown up in a household that resolutely did not discuss religion. Both of his parents were dogmatically attached to their own, and the only way of keeping harmony was to never, ever discuss it. He and his sisters had grown up with mosque on Fridays, church on Sundays, Ramadan for fasting, and Christmas for feasting. Fish on Fridays was divinity, and pork was the devil's work.

And then his mother had stopped taking her pills.

As an adult, Ashraf knew full well what had happened wasn't Mamma's fault. She'd been ill, and that was all. When his father asked for a divorce—on the grounds, unsurprisingly, of being unable to reconcile their religious beliefs—she sank into a depression and stopped taking her medication.

And without the medication, the paranoia came back. The whispers in the back of her head. The shadows of government agents in the corners of her eyes who wanted to take her away.

Ashraf knew all too well that mental health wasn't spoken of enough by Christians and Muslims alike. And his mother had been no different. Nobody but his father knew she was on the medication, and nobody at all knew that she was getting sick again.

Until the day she posted a letter to his uncle in Napoli and drove her car into the sea.

They won't take me, she'd said in that letter. *They won't take my children. I will never let them touch the children. I will deliver us all safely to the arms of Allah, and we will await you there.*

Ashraf had been nine years old. In the aftermath, he turned away from both religions. They had to both be wrong. No god at all would have allowed that to happen, he'd reasoned. His father had been furious with him, but Ashraf hadn't moved. He'd retreated into his room, into his books, into his study of human beings of history, and not emerged for almost a decade.

Until he came to the UK.

He'd been lonely, isolated, and struggling with his English in this city that talked like they had a language all of their own. He'd found himself unable to connect with the alcohol-mad culture of British students, and uninterested in the staples of their social circles—sports and sex. He got along in his classes well enough, but the moment the lecture was over, his peers would drift away.

Except for Humaira.

She'd been in his ancient art lectures, a pretty girl from Pakistan. She was a painter, doing a part-time course while her boyfriend finished his training to become an imam. When Ashraf confessed to his neglected Muslim roots, she didn't push him to go or scold him for being a bad Muslim. She'd simply said she was sorry about what had happened to his mother and told him a story of her aunt in Pakistan who'd been locked away in a room because she had seizures.

"People are crueller to each other than Allah could manage even if He wanted to, I think," she'd said, and something had shifted inside Ashraf's chest.

It wasn't Allah who'd abandoned his mother—it was people. It was people who refused to admit mental illness existed. It was people who told her to keep it quiet in case she shamed her family. It was people who'd seen chance after chance to help her and done nothing.

He'd gone back to mosque for the first time nearly a year after that conversation, with Humaira and her boyfriend, and he felt the same thing then as he did now.

That warmth that wrapped around him the moment he stepped through the doors.

Mosques were beautiful. Plain, bright shrines with the looping beauty of Arabic inscriptions on their walls. Arabic was one of the most beautiful languages in the entire world, in Ashraf's opinion. The language of songs and love and poetry. All the greatest poets had spoken Arabic; all the greatest minds had relayed their ideas in Arabic. It only made sense for the recitations to have been spoken in such a melodic, malleable tone, and it could whisper, rush, thunder, bellow through his throat and lungs when he prayed.

And in every syllable, it was warm.

It was a passionate, vibrant language, and the sounds of it spoken in a hundred accents, a thousand degrees of fluency, from the strong flow of the imam himself to the stuttering hesitations of a fourteen-year-old British lad with such a shaky grasp he could barely understand his own words, was comforting. It was like a community drawn together in a single tongue, from all the corners of the world, and Ashraf felt every last bit of tension slip free and drift away under the beating heart of his people, his god, his faith.

He prayed.

And perhaps he didn't believe that Allah created the world, or that there were mortal sins to stain their souls—but there was something here. Something otherworldly. Something powerful.

He could *feel* it, as strong as the heart in his chest.

THERE WAS A plate of casserole in the microwave when Ashraf got home.

The lights were all out, but the blue glow of the TV illuminated Jamie on the sofa, their eyes fixed on the screen. They had dragged the duvet down off the bed and turned themself into a burrito.

"What you watching?"

"Some pseudo-scientific bullshit."

"Room for one more?" Ashraf asked.

"Have your tea first," came the absent reply. "Then there's room for one more."

Ashraf ate with the plate balanced on Jamie's shins, and they watched the episode in companionable silence before he shifted to put the plate on the floor and began to tug at the duvet.

"C'mon," he coaxed. "You promised."

"I did no such thing," Jamie said but wriggled until Ashraf could open the gap and slide in behind them. They were—of course—naked.

"You're going to have to put clothes on when the winter sets in proper, you know."

"I think you'll find you have to turn the heating up," Jamie retorted. Ashraf kissed the back of their head and tucked an arm under their head to let his bicep serve as the inevitable pillow.

"What's happening?"

"This guy is stuck in a time loop, and he keeps trying to get the robot woman to teach him French."

"Is that pseudo-scientific bullshit too?"

"No, that's so ridiculous it's just become fantasy instead of sci-fi. Also, I don't like this guy. You've watched it all, right? Does he die?"

"I can't remember," Ashraf said. The warmth was beginning to drug him, and he found a flat belly under the covers and began to stroke it lightly. His thumb brushed the top of wiry hair, and he wriggled his fingers a little lower to sit in the heat between Jamie's thighs.

"If you're going to put that there, don't move."

"Got it."

He cuddled quietly until the episode was over, and once the credits started to roll, placidly allowed Jamie to rearrange them until Jamie was spread out over his chest, drowsy like a cat, and Ashraf could tuck their head under his chin and stroke their hair in long, languid movements.

"You ever wanted to grow this out?" he asked. "It'd feel nice."

"Nope," came the equally soft reply. "How was mosque?"

"Fine."

"Pray for pennies and nice weather?"

"They're like wishes; they don't come true if you tell."

"Bollocks they don't."

"You don't even know what they're called, so don't try telling me what they're about."

"I do! In the morning you have Fajr—"

"Fay-ger? What the hell is fay-ger?"

Jamie pushed up on both arms to slide higher and bit his lip. Their weight fell against Ashraf's cock, and to his surprise, a little wash of heat answered.

"Huh."

"What?"

He rolled his hips. "Bit of arousal, there."

Jamie raised their eyebrows. "Really?"

"Yeah."

"Want to do anything about it?"

"Nah." He skittered his fingers up Jamie's bare back. "Must be the shot."

"Oh sure, blame the needle, not your sinfully good-looking, incredibly fuckable, everyone-in-Newcastle-wants-a-piece-of-this partner…"

Ashraf grinned, tilting his chin up to catch another kiss. "Yeah, yeah, I know, you're stunning."

"And?"

"Gorgeous."

"And?"

"Missing your next episode."

Jamie sighed and settled back down into the cuddle.

"You'll learn one day," they complained.

"Sure," Ashraf said peaceably, resuming his stroking. "And on that day, Satan will be skating to work."

Chapter Five

ASHRAF WAS WOKEN by splinters of bright light and someone hammering on the front door.

"Shit," he mumbled and tried to move his arm. There were pins and needles in his fingers, and Jamie was a dead weight across all four limbs. "Jamie. *Jamie.* I need to get the door."

The reply might have been an instruction to commit several sins with the door, or an instruction to commit them with whoever was on the other side. Ashraf elected to ignore them and slid himself gingerly free.

Thankfully, he was still in his pyjama bottoms. So, expecting a delivery man or something similar, he didn't bother to check through the spyhole before jerking open the door.

Tariq grinned.

"Ashraf, my *man*!" he crowed and lifted his fist to bump their knuckles. "Heavy night or *heavy night*?"

"What?" Ashraf asked stupidly.

"You left this in my car," Tariq said, holding up a familiar coat. Jamie's. The pink toggles gave it away. "You never said nothing about picking up a bird."

"Yeah, well." Ashraf snatched it, coughing awkwardly. "Thanks. Uh. Kind of busy, so—"

Tariq's grin widened. "Same bird, different bird?"

The downside of mosque was Tariq. He was the worst Muslim Ashraf had ever met. He turned up one Friday in every four—and usually only after his father caused a scene at home and forced him to go—and spent the rest of his time renting women for an hour at a time, wearing a suspicious dusting of white powder under his nose, and getting into fights at nightclubs. The only thing he was good for was borrowing that nice car.

Over Ashraf's shoulder, the sofa creaked. Tariq shifted to the side and cackled with laughter. When Ashraf glanced, Jamie was stretching, their back to the door, and clad in just a T-shirt and a pair of baggy boxers. Thank God, they'd put something on when they'd gone to the bathroom last night.

"Fit," Tariq said approvingly. "Reckon she'd wear my boxers if I asked?"

Ashraf clenched his jaw. "Show some respect."

"Hey, she's hot!" Tariq threw up his hands, that shit-eating grin never faltering. "I'm just saying, if you're done with her—"

A shoulder bumped Ashraf's, and Jamie's hand snaked past him to take the coat. Their eyes raked Tariq coldly in a clear assessment, and their lip curled.

"Sorry," they said, in the highest, most cultured voice that Ashraf had ever heard come out of their lips. "I'm not into little boys. Come back when you're a real man, sweetie."

And then, incredibly obnoxiously and not something Jamie would have ordinarily have done under any circumstances, they stretched up on their toes and licked the shell of Ashraf's ear.

"I'll be in the shower, gorgeous," they purred, then turned and sashayed away towards the stairs.

Ashraf shrugged at Tariq.

"Thanks for the coat," he said. "Duty calls."

He shut the door with a snap—then put the chain on for good measure. Tariq was a prick when he was pissed off, and a pretty person he perceived to be a woman insulting his manhood was a sure-fire way to rile him up.

Ashraf followed Jamie up the stairs. They were peeling their clothes off in front of the steaming shower, and Ashraf put the lid down on the toilet before perching on it with a sigh.

"Sorry about him. You okay?"

"Yeah."

"Sure?"

Jamie shrugged. "Yeah. Not the first knobhead to call me a fit bird; won't be the last."

They stepped into the shower, and Ashraf frowned absently.

"Doesn't make it okay."

"No, but I was honestly more offended by him acting like he could have a shag with his mate's piece of meat."

"I wouldn't call us mates," Ashraf grumbled.

"You get my point, though."

Ashraf hummed. He did—but it rankled in a different way, too. Despite what everyone thought, he hadn't avoided relationships for most of his youth because he was transgender, or had issues with his body. And he wasn't asexual because he had issues with his body either. They were separate things. He was transgender, and that was a fact. He'd never been sexually attracted to a single human being in thirty-five years. That was another fact. Apart from both facts being applied to him, a single individual, they were totally unrelated.

But what he'd found when he'd come out as asexual to prospective dates was this weird expectation that either he suck it up and have sex, or he let his partner have sex with other people. Neither were acceptable, in Ashraf's eyes. He wasn't going to have sex, and especially not just because somebody else wanted him to. And he was a strictly monogamous creature. The idea of someone he adored—especially someone he adored as much as Jamie—having sex with someone else physically hurt. It ached inside.

So Tariq's smirk and swagger grated against a very different type of wound, and Ashraf found himself grinding his teeth a little as Jamie showered, turning the encounter over and over in his head.

"Will it ever bother you?" he asked eventually.

"What?"

"That we're never going to have sex?"

There it was. The flat fact. Ashraf had never seen anyone and wanted to have sex with them. He found the idea a bit daft at best, and a bit disgusting at worst. He'd never tried it, didn't want to try it, and had no intention of trying it. And the expectation of his younger years—that it was always him who ought to change and force himself to do it—was a sore point and likely always would be. He had his pride. If someone thought being regularly screwed was better than being with him, then Ashraf wanted no part of it.

But when Ashraf had told Jamie, back in their early dating days, Jamie just blinked and said, "Oh. Well. I guess I've been using toys the last couple of years. I'll just keep doing that."

Jamie scraped the water off their face and smiled out of the shower.

"Nope," they said. "I kind of have this weird requirement for sex."

"Yeah?"

"Yep. I'd want you to enjoy it. It's a crazy kink of mine."

Ashraf chuckled, some of the tension easing.

"And as you won't—" Jamie shrugged. "—then I guess we don't do it."

"You stay with me, you'll never have sex again."

"Guess not."

The flippant tone made Ashraf smile. When Jamie stepped out and wrapped themself in a towel, Ashraf reached out and towed them down onto his lap for a wet cuddle, and a wetter kiss.

"You're perfect," he said.

"Nope. We just fit."

"Yeah?"

Jamie grinned, nudging their nose against Ashraf's. "Yep. If you weren't into kisses and cuddles, then I'd be gone before you finished the sentence."

Ashraf laughed and squeezed tight. "Lucky for both of us I am, then."

"Yep." A wet kiss was buried in his beard, and Jamie squeezed tight around his neck. "Want to try carrying me down the stairs like a damsel in distress in my towel?"

"Nope. I'll trip, and we'd both end up in the hospital."

"Boring," Jamie complained, climbing off his lap. They unashamedly dropped the towel and turned their back to pluck a pair of knickers off the radiator and begin dressing.

Ashraf sat back in his damp pyjama bottoms and watched. This was when other boyfriends got aroused. Jamie naked was aesthetically gorgeous. They were all long limbs, slim frame, gentle curves, perfect skin. And he wanted to touch, feel the smooth silkiness under his palms, put his fingers and lips on the little freckles and burn lines that marked every T-shirt they'd ever worn, wanted to wrap himself around all that warmth—

But there wasn't a single trace of arousal. He'd be happier cuddling Jamie all night in front of the TV, listening to them rant and rage against bad science and refusing to admit they enjoyed the hell out of it, than having a sex marathon with a hundred orgasms in a single night.

And when Jamie turned back around, knickers on and a T-shirt hiding their braless breasts, Ashraf smiled into the kiss that was given over to him.

"Hey." Jamie's lips brushed his cheek before pulling away. "Love you."

Ashraf's heart burned.

"You too."

"Given that we crashed on the sofa, you cuddled me like I was your life support system, and we woke up all wrapped around each other," Jamie said, "we as good as had sex. So I'm going to make a hot breakfast. What d'you want?"

"Whatever," Ashraf said. "As long as we can eat it with you in my lap again."

"Gotcha." Another kiss. "Churros and chocolate, coming right up."

DESPITE IT BEING a Saturday, Ashraf went into the office anyway.

He got some of his best work done at weekends, without Kath looking daggers at him every time he mentioned his partner and students bobbing in and out all the time with daft questions. How some of them ever got into university was beyond Ashraf. Plus, Jamie was boring on Saturdays. They always disappeared to go shopping with Tabby, or off down to the beach on nice days, and while Ashraf liked Tabby well enough, she was utterly exhausting and just not his type of person.

It was the first Saturday that he'd see Jamie at all though. When they came home. All moved in and domestic.

He soldiered away with a stack of journals he needed to catch up on, liberally abusing a green highlighter and making notes in Arabic for speed. His mind could switch spoken languages at the drop of a hat, and he could keep up a conversation in mixed Arabic, Italian, and English without a problem—but his hands struggled. Flicking between English and Italian? No problem. Between either and Arabic? Major problem. The sight of the beautiful Arabic inscriptions in the mosque every Friday always seemed to reset his hands back to his mother tongue, so it was eleven o'clock before he realised he was smearing the letters by going right to left. He'd even left a note on Tom's desk that the poor man would be utterly incapable of reading.

Mind you, given Ashraf's awful handwriting in any language, maybe using Arabic wasn't any more of a barrier than using English.

Just before lunch, the flow was disturbed by footsteps in the corridor and a sharp knock on the door. Ashraf grunted, expecting the cleaners, but looked up when the door cracked open and a throat was cleared.

"Mr Callahan."

The head of department smiled genially back at him. "Hope I'm not interrupting?"

"Not—much."

"Thought I might find you here. Got ten minutes?"

"I guess." Ashraf set down the tormented highlighter. "What can I do for you?"

"This is strictly off the record," Callahan said quietly, frowning a little. He was a short, insipid-looking little man who always sported enormous bow ties and tweed suits. His receding hairline and huge round glasses didn't help. Yet he was incredibly popular with the students. Affable, friendly, and approachable, his two years as the head of department had destroyed their drop-out rate, earned them a fantastic reputation for student support and satisfaction, and reformed history as an interesting subject, not something shoved into dusty shelves and condemned to waste away. Ashraf had been to a couple of Callahan's lectures, to try to see what the magic was. For all the drab, dweeby exterior, one click into his PowerPoint slides and Callahan came alive. The passion poured off the stage and infected everyone in the room, and even the most difficult, diffident students would be hanging on his every word by the end of the hour.

But his frown looked concerned, and the back of Ashraf's neck prickled.

"There's been a—complaint."

Ashraf narrowed his eyes. "About me?"

"In a manner of speaking." Callahan waved a hand. "Between you and me, Ashraf, it's utter nonsense. It won't be upheld, and it won't be investigated, because there's nothing *to* investigate. Not only does it not meet the criteria, but I know you better than that, and as a matter of fact, I know—"

"No offence, sir, but this is more confusing than you just telling me."

Callahan snorted. "I've been informed you're in a relationship with a student."

Ashraf's fingers clenched. His teeth clacked together. A vague pinkness ghosted around the edges of his vision, then faded.

"Right," he ground out.

"It doesn't fit our criteria for an investigation," Callahan said. "If you were in the same department, then it might be a different matter. In any case, I'm going to have someone compare your teaching posts with Jamie's education record and make sure there's never been any crossover—"

"We met at debate club!" Ashraf exploded.

"I *know*."

The heavy tone and sympathetic look stopped Ashraf in his tracks.

"I *know*, mate," Callahan said quietly. "Turn it around—would you want a university to totally ignore someone saying a lecturer is having an affair with one of their students? Because that's all the complaint *is*. I know there's more to it than that, and we both know it isn't strictly true, but we have to get that down on paper before we can bin it."

"So it's a formal complaint, then?"

"Not as such," Callahan said awkwardly. "I got a note in the internal post. I have to be able to point to some action and say we looked into it and there was nothing there."

"You know there's nothing there," Ashraf snapped. "They're not my student."

"I know."

"We met at debate club, not a lecture."

"I know that, too."

"They're an adult. They're doing a PhD. They're not some naïve little freshman who's just left home for the first time."

"I *know*."

"It's been nearly six months, Chris!"

Callahan took his glasses off, sighing. "I know all of this," he said. "I think it's bollocks. Not only are you incapable of even coercing Dawn to book the good theatre for your lectures, Professor Hanley is a right bastard if he even thinks anyone's taking advantage of his students. He might be a walking health and safety hazard at the best of times, but he's perceptive. If he even thought for a second something untoward was going on, I've no doubt you'd have had an irate Scot storming into one of your lectures and beating you to death with the microphone."

Ashraf raised his eyebrows at the colourful image. "Has...that happened?"

"It didn't quite get that far, but only because his lab assistants intervened," Callahan said. "There was an incident a few years ago. One of the biology department staff made some distinctly inappropriate remarks to his girlfriend in Hanley's hearing. Girlfriend happened to be one of Hanley's masters' students, and Hanley nearly decked him. Complete mess."

Ashraf whistled, and made a mental note to be the most perfect partner in the universe in front of Professor Hanley.

"I just need to be able to document that we looked into it, that's all," Callahan said. "I don't think there's anyone to be worried about. Are you worried we'll uncover anything?"

"No," Ashraf said tightly.

"Then it'll all blow over. We just need to be able to say we did our duty in case this isn't a one-off complaint."

"You mean in case someone's got it out for me. For us."

Because Ashraf knew full well who it was.

"Fact is, you're vulnerable to this sort of accusation," Callahan said quietly.

They stared at one another in silence, the reasons echoing like ghosts between them. They both knew why.

"Just mind out," Callahan said. "Don't give anyone any ammunition to use against you."

"Am I being investigated?"

"Not formally."

"So I am."

"I'll need to talk to Jamie, I expect. Have a look at your respective records with the university. Have a word with student support, see if Jamie's ever approached them with any issues. If we find nothing, then that'll be the end of it."

"Will it go on my record?"

"Not if there's nothing to substantiate it."

"Which there isn't."

Callahan bowed his head in a non-committal fashion.

"This conversation didn't happen, did it?" Ashraf snapped.

"I'd...prefer if it didn't, no."

"Right."

"Ashraf."

Ashraf pursed his lips and glanced up from his furious perusal of his scratchy notes.

"I believe you," Callahan said. "I just need to be able to prove I'm right."

Chapter Six

JAMIE WAS ALREADY home when Ashraf arrived.

Tabby had been over, judging by the wine glasses on the coffee table and the empty KFC bag in the bin, but the house was starting to fill with the enticing smell of spicy beef enchiladas. Jamie was dancing around the kitchenette with their headphones on, swaying to some inaudible tune in one of Ashraf's T-shirts and nothing else at all.

Ashraf swallowed.

"Hey!" The greeting was shouted, then the headphones came off and a kiss landed on Ashraf's chin. "Ellie had the baby this morning, so Mam says we should go up in two or three weeks. Tabby says hi, and Shane sort of grunts in your direction because he's shy—I'm going hiking up the coast with them both next week if you want to join us, last of autumn before it gets grim and shit. And dinner's in fifteen, you hungry?"

"Okay, hi to them both, probably not, and a little bit?"

He was hungry for something else, too, and he reached for a cuddle. Jamie squeaked as they were folded into a tight squeeze, and laughed breathlessly.

"Hell-*o*. Is this good-day cuddles, or—"

Ashraf buried his face into Jamie's shoulder.

"Oh, *bad*-day cuddles, I gotcha." A hand stroked through the hair at the nape of his neck. "What's up?"

"Kath's put in a complaint."

"Kath as in your office buddy?"

"Yeah."

"What about—you been eating fish tacos at work or something?"

Ashraf didn't laugh. "About you and me."

Jamie paused.

Then: "Sorry, what?"

"She's complained to Callahan that I'm dating a student."

Jamie muttered something uncomplimentary and wriggled free.

"*A* student," they said tartly. "Not *your* student."

"That's what I said," Ashraf grumbled. "He thinks it won't go anywhere, but I'm pissed off."

"Well, yeah."

"I knew she felt funny about it, but to go to my boss?"

"So she's either homophobic, racist, or both."

Ashraf snorted. "Yeah, well. Last time we talked about it, she was all about how you're twelve years younger than me, and you're queer."

"And you're Muslim."

"She didn't say—"

"But she's thinking it," Jamie said softly. "I'm a poor vulnerable white girl, and you're—"

They trailed off. Bile hit the back of Ashraf's throat. Yeah, he'd been in the UK long enough to see the papers. Rotherham. Rochdale. Oxford. Newcastle. Gangs of Muslim men grooming white teenagers for sex. Their faces all across the rags, their crimes used to target mosques and taxi firms, takeaways and market stalls. He never thought Kath had bought into any of it, never thought she'd be that awful to believe the tabloids, but—

But Jamie was right. If they had been a twenty-three-year-old girl from Egypt, from Iraq, from Pakistan, then Kath wouldn't have batted an eyelash.

"Fuck," Ashraf ground out. "Fuck her. Just—fuck her."

He rarely swore, and Jamie's surprised expression eased some of the tension.

"Hey. It doesn't matter. Callahan believes you. And they can't do shit anyway. I'm legal, it's legal, and if they start asking me if I'm being taken advantage of, I'm going to start laughing in their faces."

Ashraf smiled wanly.

"C'mon." Jamie rubbed their hands up Ashraf's arms. "Enchiladas and a good cuddle. We have another two episodes to get through before bed, and Tabby didn't drink all her wine, so I'm going to get drunk and giggly again, and you're going to pull faces at me and love me anyway. *And* George texted and said they've booked the place we're staying in Aqaba, so we need to check flights and make sure to get you a seat on the same ones. Busy evening, right?"

Ashraf snuck another hug at the counter, blowing against Jamie's neck until they squirmed.

"Yeah," he said, "but can we sort flights and the christening and everything tomorrow? Think I need TLC first, and plans later."

"No problem."

Ashraf watched the enchiladas get carefully slid out of the pan onto salad-laden plates, and wished he could think of what the hell he was supposed to say to Kath now.

HE DIDN'T SAY anything at all to Kath.

By Monday, the anger had died to a simmering frustration, and he decided to simply not be in the office at all. He and Jamie would be going to Edinburgh for the christening on the first weekend in November. And they'd be gallivanting off to Jordan in mid-December over the Christmas break. He didn't need to be wound up about Kath.

It was easier said than done, but Ashraf took to avoiding the office as much as possible, doing more of his research and prep at home or in the library. It helped that he still had to take his own seminars, and he could spend more time in various classrooms trying to get first years to understand that history didn't begin when people learned to write.

Of course, they didn't talk to Ashraf about the complaint formally.

They just talked to Jamie.

Jamie met him after his last lecture on Thursday in a towering temper. Jamie was usually very calm and peaceful, but when they got angry, they went nuclear. It was almost scary the first time Ashraf saw it, and he feared the day when he'd be the cause, and the explosion happened right in his face, but at least the signs were obvious. When he came out of the lecture hall, Jamie was sitting on his bike, kicking the wall savagely with their shoes and scowling down at their phone, texting furiously.

"Everything okay?" Ashraf asked warily.

"No."

The word was short, sharp, and succinct.

"Right," Ashraf said and gripped the bike saddle either side of Jamie's bum. "Hey." His face was very close at that range, but Jamie didn't look up. "Want to go to the cafe at the end of the road and get one of their ridiculous slabs of cake?"

"Chocolate fudge. Warm. With cream." Jamie got off the bike only to put one foot up on the frame by the back wheel.

"Okay. Hang on properly, though."

Jamie rarely rode behind him. Ashraf felt oddly young like that, but Jamie's grip on his shoulders wasn't exactly kid-friendly. He rode slowly, using the pavement rather than the road, and coasted to a stop beside the cafe rather than braking properly.

It wasn't their usual spot—too expensive—but the cake was top quality and could hand over diabetes and a stroke inside a single slab. It was Jamie's go-to feel-good place. Ashraf wordlessly handed them a tenner and raised his eyebrows when it was met with a scowl.

"I got dragged into a meeting with Hanley and Callahan and some idiot from student support," Jamie said and snatched the tenner. "They wanted to ask all sorts about our private life. I want to *strangle* Kath."

Ashraf winced but didn't say anything until they were situated in a corner, steaming cups of tea between them, and a brick of Jamie's beloved cake oozing melted chocolate and whipped cream onto a fancy plate.

Then he said, "What happened?"

"Told you. Got dragged into a meeting. They started asking all these super personal questions. Like how often we had sex, if you bought me gifts a lot, if you'd asked me to move in with you, if you were controlling—"

Ashraf dropped his face into his hand and swore in Italian.

"I was trying to be helpful at first, like I told them how we met and that you're coming to meet my family at the christening, and I kept pointing out we're nothing to do with each other professionally, and it's a coincidence we're both at the university, we could have met in a coffee shop or anywhere—"

"What did Hanley do?"

"Nothing. I think he thought it was all crap too, to be honest."

"Good."

"And Callahan was super awkward and kept apologising for being intrusive, but *God*, the woman from student support…"

"Bad?"

"You'd have thought I was some little kid who didn't know what a dick was," Jamie fumed. Then, quite suddenly, they sagged. Like all the fight had gone out of them, they sagged back in their chair and began to go pink. "I'm sorry."

"What?"

"I'm really, really sorry."

Ashraf frowned and reached across the table to touch their wrist. "Jamie?"

"I didn't—I didn't *mean* to, it just slipped out, they kept asking on and on and on about—"

The flush was centring in their cheeks. Their bottom lip and voice started to shake. Ashraf's heart lurched.

"Don't *cry*—"

"I outed you."

Jamie blurted it out and then covered their face. Ashraf blinked, stunned.

"You outed me?"

"I didn't mean to!"

Jamie was crying. He could hear it. Jamie was crying behind their hands.

"She just kept asking about sex, about how you initiated it and if you ever bought me anything in exchange for it and when we first did it and I just—I was getting so angry at her, I just blurted out we'd never done it, and she looked at me like, *yeah right sure*, and I said it. I'm sorry, I know I shouldn't have done it, it just *happened*—"

The air rushed back out of Ashraf's lungs, and he got up. Dragged his chair around to Jamie's side of the little table. Sat down.

And tugged Jamie's shaking body into his arms.

"Hey," he murmured, burying them in a cuddle and rocking them lightly. "Hey, it's okay. It's okay. I'd be really upset if you'd outed me as trans, but not as ace. I doubt Hanley even cares. Callahan isn't going to say anything. And the support woman can't; she's the one who'll have swallowed the HR handbook and all the rest of it. It doesn't matter."

Jamie unfolded enough to cling, burying their face in his shoulder.

"It's all right," Ashraf said soothingly, rubbing their back. "I get what happened. I probably would have told them too, under the circumstances. And you're sorry for not asking first, so it's fine. It's fine, Jamie, it *is*."

He'd never seen Jamie cry before, and he wasn't sure how long it ought to take for them to stop. He simply held on, pitching his voice low and trying to comfort. Had Jamie outed him as trans, then that might have been a different matter. He'd worked hard to pass, was proud of passing, and it was such a deeply, intensely private thing to him that he didn't like to talk about it, even with people who by their own nature would understand, like Jamie.

But being ace? He'd never struggled with that the way he'd struggled with being trans. He just *was*. He'd never felt ashamed of it, never felt he ought to try and change it, never felt inferior or even very different because of it. He'd always thought the problem was with everybody else, being mad about partners and romance and all that nauseating rubbish. He'd never missed having a partner until Jamie wriggled into his life, and would miss *Jamie*, not being a boyfriend, if Jamie were to go again. Even if Jamie raised a question mark over being aromantic, they hadn't raised one over being asexual.

So he meant it when he pressed his lips against Jamie's ear and whispered that it was fine.

"M'still sorry," Jamie mumbled when the tears had abated and they squirmed sideways in his hold to speak against his neck.

"I know." Ashraf smoothed down a bit of their hair. "And I forgive you. So we're good. Okay?"

"M'kay."

"Like I said, if I was being grilled under pressure about why we're not in some weird coercive relationship, I might well have pointed out that you're more likely to try and push me into sex than the other way around."

"Wouldn't."

"Yeah, I know, dumped on your arse if I thought you would," Ashraf chided gently. "But if one of us were going to push to have sex, it *would* be you. Given you like it and I don't."

"Yeah. S'pose."

"You all right?"

Jamie shook their head. Ashraf sighed, kissing their temple.

"Yeah, I guess not. You might feel better if you finish your cake, though. Then you can tell them I bought you cake to stop you crying, and student support would really flip their shit."

Jamie chuckled wetly. "You bought me cake *before* the crying."

"Good point. Want another cup of tea, then? Restock all the water you just lost?"

"Hot chocolate. Please."

"Okay." Ashraf squeezed one last time before letting go and fishing in his jacket for his wallet. At the counter, he glanced over his shoulder while the machine hissed away, and saw Jamie mop themself up with a tissue and start in on the cake again. By the time Ashraf got back, the only sign of the crying was a slight pinkness in their face and a croaky voice.

"Thanks."

"Take it we're going home for a fleece cuddle after this?"

"Yeah."

"And you have to tell me all your plans for Jordan."

That earned him a little bit of a smile.

"Well, I'll be going out diving almost every day. But afterwards, just—lounge around the hotel pool. Beach. Maybe do a day trip up to Petra. I've always wanted to see Petra."

Ashraf agreed absently. Beach. He hadn't been on a beach in decades. For a moment, his stomach clenched—then he exhaled, and relaxed again. It would be fine. Just a load of sand and some umbrellas. Wasn't like he had to get in the water.

"Hey. Isn't your mum from Jordan?"

"What? No. Egypt."

"Oh, sorry—"

Ashraf shrugged. "I've only been to Egypt when I was a little kid. Never Jordan. It'll be an adventure."

"Bet you'll go really brown."

"Yep."

"Do they speak the same language?"

"They both speak Arabic. Different dialects, though, so I don't know how much I'll be able to manage with the locals. I don't know if there's another language in Jordan."

"Then how do you know they speak Arabic?"

"It's the language of Islam."

"It has a whole language?"

Ashraf rolled his eyes. "I have *got* to get you an introduction to Islam book."

"Or you could just tell me," Jamie said snottily. Literally. They blew their nose into the tissue and offered him a wan smile. "Sorry. I know I'm an ignorant shit sometimes."

Ashraf shrugged.

"I can learn, though."

"You'll learn next Ramadan, all right. I'm not having you making those casseroles in the house when I can't eat."

"Why do you even do Ramadan? I mean..." Jamie waved a hand between them. "Kinda huge sin right here, right?"

"Why do you christen babies in a church when you're a bigger atheist than Richard Dawkins?"

Jamie opened their mouth—then closed it again with a laugh.

"Point taken."

Ashraf raised his cup in a 'cheers' gesture.

"I like it when you speak Arabic, though."

"Do you?"

"Uh-huh. I listen to your prayers."

Ashraf blushed.

"It sounds beautiful."

"It is," Ashraf said. "It's a wonderful language. All the great poets spoke and wrote in Arabic. I'll have to dig out some of them for you—you'd probably like some of Abu Nuwas' raunchier work. Humaira—you know, the imam's wife—she reckons he might have been gay."

"Oh, is he a modern poet?"

"Mm, no, not quite."

"Was it allowed to be gay back then?"

"Doubt it," Ashraf said.

"Can I get it in English?"

Ashraf groaned. "I'll translate them for you, but the original sounds more beautiful. I'll read you that as well."

Jamie smiled. It wasn't quite their megawatt beam, but it was a good deal better than tears.

"Can you do that tonight?"

"Eh?"

"Look some up and read to me?"

"TLC?"

"Yeah."

Ashraf slid an arm around their shoulders and tugged them in for another hug. They sagged into him placidly, and he rubbed his nose against the crown of their head.

"'Course I can," he said. "Good cuddle, bit of poetry, maybe some TV so you can feel superior and make fun of the show writers, and I'll even cook."

"Uh, no thanks, I like life."

"Oi!"

The next smile was a real one, followed by a chocolate-flavoured kiss and a nose nudging against the side of his own.

"Takeaway? Pizza from Papa Romeo's?"

Ashraf squeezed tight and then nudged them back towards the cake. "Deal. Get that down you, then let's go."

Chapter Seven

ASHRAF SLAMMED INTO the office, dumped his folders on the table, and turned on Kath.

"Are you *quite* fucking finished?" he shouted.

Kath blinked up at him around her cereal bar. Slowly, she broke it off, put it aside, and swallowed with an unhealthy wrenching sound.

"Are you talking to me?"

"Who else would I be talking to?"

"Ash, mate." Tom looked up from his study of a dusty tome. "You want to try English?"

Ashraf blew out through his nose in a gusty snort. Of course. He'd reverted to Italian.

"Are," he said carefully, snapping his teeth around the edges of the English words, "you quite. *Fucking*. Finished?"

Kath blinked. "I'm sorry?"

"Jamie got dragged into a meeting with student support, and I got a grilling from Callahan because someone reported our relationship as inappropriate. They were in tears yesterday!"

"And you think *I* did it?"

"You're the only one around here with a problem!"

She pursed her lips and dropped her gaze. "I'm sorry if Jamie was upset."

"They were in tears," Ashraf snapped. "As it happens, both Callahan and Hanley think it's a load of shit, because it is. What the hell is your problem?"

"I'm sorry if—"

"No." Ashraf held up a hand. "Stop right there. Are you sorry or aren't you? No ifs, no buts, just that. Are you sorry?"

She frowned. "I'm not sorry for acting to make sure that—"

"So why did you feel the need?" Ashraf snapped. "Jamie's a PhD student. They're twenty-three. They aren't *my* student, and I'm a lecturer, not a professor."

"It—"

"It isn't inappropriate even by the university's standards, so why were you worried, Kath? Because they're queer, or because I'm Muslim?"

There was a sharp silence. Kath's jaw sagged. They could have heard a pin drop in Jamie's beloved Australia.

"Did you get anxious because it was an older Muslim man going after a young white queer person?"

"I don't know what you're trying to insinuate, but—"

"You said yourself LGBT people are vulnerable."

"They *are.*"

"Did you not consider maybe I'm LGBT myself?"

Her eyes widened, and Ashraf bit back on a vicious sense of schadenfreude. Of course she hadn't. He was brown and Muslim. Jamie was very plainly AFAB. He was just a straight Muslim guy in his thirties, going after a much younger vulnerable white girl. Just like what was always being plastered all over the racist tabloids, every hour of every damn day.

The English, Italian, and Arabic phrases for fuck you jostled for room in his brain.

Something slammed. "Who wants coffee?" Tom asked very loudly, rocketing up from his chair. He grabbed his jacket, then Ashraf's elbow, and shoved him towards the door. "Come on, pal, give us a hand. Usual, Kath? Brilliant!"

And then the office door was closed behind them before Ashraf had a moment to think.

"Christ," Tom said, shoving his hands in his pockets and kicking the back of Ashraf's shoe to make him start walking. "Come on. You need to cool off. What the hell was all that about?"

Ashraf explained in a voice so tight it threatened to break. About Callahan's meeting, about Jamie being dragged into one of their own, about the intrusive questions, about—although not the technical reason for—Jamie crying in the cafe.

"So that's what did it," Tom mused. "Jamie cried, you exploded. I've never seen you angry before, mate."

"Wouldn't you be angry?"

"'Course I would," Tom said flatly. As they stepped out into the cold, he hunched his shoulders. "I'm just saying, I don't reckon she's done it because she's ra—"

"Don't tell me what people do and don't do because they are or aren't racist," Ashraf retorted.

Tom—wisely—closed his mouth.

"I'm going to ask admin to shift me into a different office."

"Ash, c'mon—"

"No. I'm not working in there with her anymore. She thinks I'm preying on Jamie like some perv."

Tom coughed uncomfortably. "Are they, uh. Well. You know. Actually...investigating?"

"Callahan says it's not a formal complaint; it's just so they look like they did something. He doesn't believe it."

"Good."

Ashraf threw him a look.

"Hey, *I* don't believe it," Tom said. "I've met he—er, them. They've got you wrapped round their little finger."

Ashraf grunted.

As they passed into the humid warmth of the coffee shop round the corner, Tom shifted from foot to foot. "What did you mean by you're LGBT as well?"

"Exactly what it sounded like," Ashraf said shortly.

Tom pinked. "Yeah, but...uh...you're into women. Aren't you?"

Ashraf clenched his jaw. "No."

"No?" Tom squeaked. "So you're—you're into blokes?"

"No."

Tom blinked. "Wait. You're—wait. How can you be into neither? How can you be LGBT and into neither?"

Ashraf snorted and stepped back from the counter. "Screw this. I'm working from home today."

"Ash!"

"Try spelling it out!" he shouted over his shoulder as he pushed his way out of the coffee shop and back into the cold.

Working from home, he texted Jamie. *Where are you?*

Jamie: *Was just about to head out to the labs. Want to come with and lurk asexily in a corner while I look stupid in my white coat and massive goggles? I'll even blow you kisses over a Bunsen burner if you're really lucky! xxx*

Just that like, the tension and anger started to ease. Jamie being daft was the solution to all of life's problems, in Ashraf's opinion.

Ashraf: *I'm feeling lucky. Meet you outside the library and we can walk down?*

Jamie: *Yep! Getting the bus, see you in twenty, love you xxx*

Ashraf rolled his head back to stare at the grey sky, and let it all out in one long, cathartic breath. Jamie would make him feel better. Jamie *always* made him feel better.

"SO YOU ENDED up coming out anyway?" Jamie asked.

Ashraf had stopped by the office only to retrieve his things and then set himself up on an empty bench in the lab. Hanley's PhD students had free use of it whenever the building was open, and all the undergraduates were in lectures, so the place was quiet.

"Basically," Ashraf said, not looking up from his marking. "He's dense, but he's not thick. He'll work it out."

"The ace bit or—" Jamie glanced over at Meg, the only other person in the room. She was bent over her microscope, a pair of enormous headphones broadcasting the tinny echoes of death metal in the lab. "—the trans bit?"

"Both, probably."

"Are you okay with that?"

Ashraf sighed, straightening up and propping his chin on his hand.

"No," he admitted. "I mean, about the trans part. I didn't transition so I could go around telling everyone I didn't always have the junk I have now."

"Excuse me, it's not junk. It's magnificent. And more than a little bit intimidating. You could model budgie smugglers with that tackle. If you were into it, I'd be all over that."

Ashraf coughed an embarrassed laugh.

"You do realise," Jamie said in a low voice, "that he'll probably think you're a trans *woman*."

"What?"

"Tom."

"Why—"

Jamie raised their eyebrows and made a gesture at their chin. Ashraf blinked, scratching at his beard.

"Seriously?"

"Um, *yeah*. He's not going to believe your birth certificate for a minute."

Ashraf snorted, smirking a little. Ten years since he'd started passing and he still felt that strange rush of pride whenever someone said something like that.

"We could break him in gently with you," Jamie said, "and then once he's got his mind around that, upgrade him to me. Let's see him look up androphilia on the internet."

"Please don't. He'll be showing me porn clips for weeks."

Jamie grinned over the top of their equipment, and Ashraf was struck with a soft, warm feeling in his chest. He suddenly wanted to kiss them.

"Thanks."

"For what?"

"Making light of it," Ashraf admitted. "Think I needed someone to tell me I'm overreacting."

"About Kath? You're not. About Tom? Yeah, maybe you are a little. I mean, he's nice, but he has the social skills of a Neanderthal. It's not really that fair to expect someone like Tom to be all clued up on human beings. Modern ones, anyway."

"That's a gross insult to Neanderthals. They were clever and capable of both logical and creative thinking. You take that back."

"All right, all right." Jamie rolled their eyes, flashing Ashraf another bright smile. "God, you're in a mood. Do *you* need cake at that cafe?"

"Both of us to be finished with work and going home, maybe."

"Not for ages yet, sorry." Jamie pulled a face. "Look on the bright side, you can always ask for a different office, right? Or maybe you've made her uncomfortable enough that she will."

"I'm going to ask. But unless someone wants to swap, there's not much chance of it."

"No?"

"No room." Ashraf sighed, still tugging at his beard. "I don't know. I can't let it slide—if you were dating Tom, she'd not have had a problem—but I don't want to stir everything up. And now, coming out to Tom will have only complicated things, and—"

"Hey."

Jamie's voice had dropped again. They moved around the lab table and came to perch on the very edge of the bench where Ashraf was working.

"Gimme those."

Ashraf gave up his hands to be held in Jamie's lap. Those dark eyes were sombre but gentle.

"Go to mosque."

"Think I ought to?"

"I think you're wound up and annoyed, and you always calm down after prayers. Go to mosque. Stay as long as you need. And when you're done, go home, and I'll either be there or meet you there, and we can have an evening in. Sound good?"

Ashraf exhaled and leaned forward for a short, chaste kiss. Jamie was right. He'd gotten too used to working in a small environment without—he thought—much exposure to Islamophobia. He was out of practice at his coping techniques.

"Sounds good."

Chapter Eight

HE TOOK TO doing most of his research from home.

The upside of lecturing was that he only *had* to be in the office during his office hours, which were two hours on Tuesday afternoons. Otherwise, he could do everything elsewhere. The library, home, cafes with free Wi-Fi, wherever he pleased. The joys of modern technology.

So Ashraf made a new habit of it until he could figure out what to do about Kath. He wanted to forgive and forget, pass it over, be mature enough to accept that she'd been stupid but not really that malicious about it, that it was a prejudice she probably didn't even realise she had.

But the other part of him—the kid that had grown up Muslim in Christian Italy, the teenager who'd been asked if his mother had blown herself up in that car, the student who'd been jumped on his way back from mosque one night—couldn't forget. He saw the headlines every day, of evil gangs of Muslim thugs preying on little white girls. He saw the TV think pieces on Islam being a violent religion that lent itself to radicalisation. He saw the uneasy looks on the train if he had the wire of his headphones sticking out of his pocket. He'd grown up being hated for being a Muslim, and part of him couldn't forget. Kath had seen him just how the *Daily Mail* and Channel 4 wanted her to see him. Not as an anthropology lecturer, a charity supporter, a science fiction fan, a *person* who was in *love*.

As a predator.

So he avoided her and the office as much as humanly possible, went to mosque twice a week instead of once to clear his mind better, and watched November roll over the city in grey fogs, endless downpours, and bitter cold. Cycling to work got worse, coffee got better, and the first of the tedious Christmas jingles started to sound on the radio in the kitchenette.

Winter had arrived.

And with winter came the christening. The first Friday in November, Ashraf came home from mosque to a couple of backpacks by the door and rose from Fajr in the morning to Jamie sliding blindly from the bed, hair a mess and bare body beautiful as always, to disappear into the bathroom.

"Is it too late to bail?" Ashraf called through the closed door.

"Yes!"

He grimaced and went downstairs to make breakfast.

"CAN YOU GIVE me *any* warning what I'm walking into?" Ashraf asked as they climbed onto the bus, not a hundred yards from the train station. Jamie led him to the back with a chuckle, and he found himself forced into the window seat, peering out at a grey Edinburgh that was threatening rain.

Didn't look too dissimilar to Newcastle, actually.

"Well, not really. She'll like you fine."

"You said she wasn't really expecting me. What *was* she expecting?"

Jamie rolled their eyes. "Expecting, or hoping for?"

"Both?"

"Expecting, some druggie dropout idiot who was going to get me knocked up and then piss off."

Ashraf blinked. "Uh. What?"

"That's what my old man was, that's what my nieces' dads are. It's just—the type of guy that the type of girl round our way ends up with. But then, I wasn't expected to end up at university doing a PhD."

"How did you?"

"Graft." Jamie shrugged. "I didn't set out to, you know. I just—loved the sea. *Loved* it. And my biology teacher in school said I had potential and pushed me, so...I ended up sticking with it, instead of going and working in a shop like Ellie."

"Ahh."

"So once I went to uni, Mam started telling me to find myself a law student or a doctor, somebody who'd be rich in ten years."

Ashraf whistled. "Well, you chose wrong."

"Mm, don't think I did," Jamie said, grinning. "Anyway, she'll like you."

"Why?"

"Because I like you."

"And it's really that easy?"

"Well, don't steal from her or drop-kick the baby out of a window. But I kind of figured you're not into that, so..."

Ashraf groaned. Jamie just grinned.

"At least tell me something so I'm not totally lost."

"Don't mention my dad."

"Bad news?"

"Scummy news. It's been just me and Mam and Ellie and Izzy since I was about...seven? Eight? Long enough, anyway."

"And Izzy and Ellie are your sisters?"

"Yep."

"Older, younger."

"Both older. Izzy's in the army—you won't meet her, she couldn't get away. Ellie has two kids—Sammy and the new baby, Suzette. Sammy's four."

"Sammy's a girl?"

"So far," Jamie said cheerily. "Ellie's a shop girl. Mam looks after the kids most of the time."

"Guessing their dad isn't around?"

"Dads. And nope, neither of them. Between you and me, I don't think Ellie even knows who Suzette's dad is, and Sammy's was as shit as ours, so they're better off without him."

Ashraf blew upwards into his hair. "This is complicated."

"Excuse me, I didn't go and live with my aunt and uncle and fifty billion cousins."

"I don't have fifty billion cousins," Ashraf protested.

"No, only thirty-eight."

Ashraf waited a long minute before saying, "Thirty-nine." Just to get Jamie to roll their eyes and elbow him in the stomach.

The bus was the local type. It weaved through the estates, round corners housing little shops and tiny barbers, and past rows upon rows of parked cars and women pushing buggies. People got on and off at every stop, carrying shopping or dressed in supermarket uniforms. A nurse was whistling to herself loudly at the front. And Jamie—knees spread and feet together, lounging back in their seat with one earphone in, hat jammed low over their ears but letting a tuft of hair go free over their forehead—fitted right in. With their odd combination of skinny jeans and too-large leather jacket, they looked irrepressibly young and obnoxiously casual, like they thought they owned the place.

Ashraf couldn't help it—he lifted an arm over the back of Jamie's seat and lounged alongside them, earning himself a surprised smile and a knee nudging against his own.

"See?" Jamie said. "You got this."

Ashraf let them assume what they wanted.

Then the bus rolled around yet another corner, and Jamie beamed, jabbing the bell with a thumb. The bus stopped in the middle of a row of council houses, obviously so by their loveless doors, the tatty green around them, and the identical gates and fences to every front door as far as the eye could see. Old toys and bikes were everywhere. A plastic bag fluttered in a dead tree, and a pair of trainers had been flung over a telephone wire. Cars were a mix of flash BMWs on the latest plates and scabby Peugeots on plates that were older than Ashraf's *dad*. And everyone seemed to be home.

Ashraf swallowed uneasily.

Jamie, though, wore the brightest smile in the world. They bounced off down the pavement, and Ashraf hurried to keep up. He hunched his shoulders as a man smoking in his doorway paused mid-drag to scowl. Bitterly, he reflected that he ought to have borrowed Tariq's car after all.

Jamie's mum's house was the next street over. It was identical to all the other houses: battered front door, missing gate, weeds abundant in the box of a front garden. The windows looked grubby, and the bins were overflowing. Ashraf could feel the hairs on the back of his neck beginning to stand on end.

Then Jamie jammed a key in the lock, kicked the door, and popped it open.

"Mam!" they shouted.

"Eeee!"

The squeal was alarming. Ashraf jumped, hesitating on the threshold as a fat woman in fluffy slippers and a baggy tank top showing a stretched, old tattoo on her upper arm came hurrying down the narrow hall. She clapped her hands around Jamie's neck, kissed their cheek, and dragged them into a fierce hug.

"There you are!" she crooned. Then she let go and slapped their arm. "Where've you been, eh? Never visit your old mam, you don't!"

"I visited when I got back from Australia!"

"Tha' were two months ago, don't you cheek me!"

Jamie looked nothing like their mother. The smile was similar, Ashraf supposed, but little else: she was very tall and very wide, more like a building than anyone's mother. The telltale stains of cigarettes lay on her fingers and teeth. Her hair was dyed a ferocious metallic red, but her baggy clothes and slippers were quiet and understated. Her voice was loud, but the accent soft. The *thwack* of her hand on Jamie's jacket was muffled, even if the motion had looked brutal.

And then she clucked her tongue at Ashraf and said, "Tea? Tea."

Ashraf blinked as she vanished into the back of the house, and Jamie laughed at his expression.

"Come on, then," they said.

The back of the house contained a kitchen. It was tiny but pristine and cosy. A table had been rammed into a corner with two chairs, both laden with cushions. There was barely any counter space, but three layers of shelves on all the walls were overflowing with pots, pans, and packets. Stew was bubbling on the stove, and a radio was bawling— of all things—The Proclaimers.

It was nothing like the grubby, sparse outdoors. Ashraf stared around the warm, welcoming space, and relaxed.

"Ellie will be round in ten minutes or so with the wee ones, and then we'll be off out," Mrs Singer—*was* she Mrs Singer? Jamie hadn't mentioned if their parents had been married—said, rummaging teabags out of boxes and milk out of the fridge. She moved quickly, almost jerkily, and Ashraf revised his earlier opinion. She had none of Jamie's looks, but her mannerisms were intimately familiar. He felt like he'd seen her brew a thousand cups before.

"Is she bringing the pancake?" Jamie asked, leaning up against the sink. Ashraf took one of the kitchen chairs. Something furry rubbed his ankle, and he peered under the table to see a skinny black cat staring curiously up at him.

"Away with you! Pancake, honestly—you can't be calling her pancake!"

"Why not?"

Ashraf patted his knee, and the cat jumped up. It sniffed at his jumper and then began to purr.

"Because she's a gorgeous little girl, not a pancake."

"But—"

"No arguments! You ought to know better."

"What, calling a baby a pancake or arguing with you?"

"Oi! Cheeky shit. There!"

A mug of tea banged down in front of him, and Ashraf jumped violently. The cat shot away into the hall, and Mrs Singer slammed herself down in the chair opposite him with a throaty laugh.

"So you're this—professor. Ashraf, wasn't it?"

"I'm a lecturer. I haven't got a professorship," Ashraf said hastily.

"University's university, isn't it?" she quipped. "Never went meself. Jamie's the first of ours. What do you lecture, then?"

"Uh, anthropology."

"You what, love?"

Jamie laughed. "History of mankind, Mam."

"I know that! I'm no' thick," she said, squinting at Ashraf. "You're a quiet one, aren't you?"

"Er. Sorry."

She snorted, her eyes narrowing even further. "Jamie's not told me a thing about you. Where're you from, then? That's no Geordie accent."

Ashraf chuckled. "No, definitely not. I'm from Terracina."

"Where?"

"Italy."

"You're Italian?" She raised her eyebrows, her gaze scanning his face. "Bit dark for that, aren't you?"

"Mam!"

Ashraf pulled a face. "Not really. It's near Napoli."

"You what?"

"Naples. Uh, Pompeii."

"Oh, with that mountain and them ruins and whathaveyou."

"Yeah," he said. "My mother was from Egypt, though."

Her eyebrows rose even further and met her red hair. "Isn't that full of Muslims?"

His stomach clenched. Again. This again. "It's a Muslim country, yes," he said warily. First Kath, now Jamie's mum?

"You a Muslim or a Christian, then?"

He swallowed. "Muslim."

She opened her mouth—and then keys rattled, and the front door banged.

"Mam!"

Mrs Singer flew up from the table, abandoning her tea in a heartbeat. Jamie quietly crossed the little kitchen and stooped to kiss the crown of Ashraf's head.

"You okay? You look funny."

"Is this going to be a problem?" Ashraf asked tightly.

"What?"

"My faith."

"Your f—oh! Oh, no, no—I'm sorry." Jamie grimaced. "I'm sorry, pet—she's just nosy. She won't have an issue with it, I promise."

"How do you know?"

"She's not like that," Jamie said. "Hey. *Hey*. She's not."

"Then why would she ask?"

"Um." Jamie pinked a little. "She, uh. She's probably worried you're not...queer friendly."

Ashraf stared blankly.

"As in, you think I'm just your girlfriend."

"Oh. *Oh*. Because of my faith?"

"Potentially, yeah. And that you'd have a problem with it. With me. And she doesn't like people sniffing round her family who're going to have problems with who they are."

Ashraf laughed in a flood of relief. "That's it? That's why she was asking?"

"Yeah."

"Well," he said, twisting around in his chair to reach out and snag Jamie's wrist, towing them in for a hug. He pressed a kiss to their stomach through the fluffy shield of their jumper—or rather, his jumper that they'd appropriated from him months ago. "I think we can safely say that I'll pass muster on that one."

"Would you be okay telling her?"

"That I'm not exactly the poster child of cisgender heterosexuality myself?"

"Yeah."

He hummed. "I'm not sure yet. Ace, okay. Let me think about the gender thing."

Jamie kissed the top of his head. "You got it. I'll drop the ace thing nice and subtle, like."

Ashraf opened his mouth to pour scorn on the idea of Jamie having ever been subtle a day in their life, but the moment was broken by a delighted shriek from the hall and the pitter-patter of tiny feet.

Or rather, the loud clumping stomps of a miniature elephant.

"Ankle Jamie, Ankle Jamie!"

"Sammy!"

Sammy was a tornado with frizzy brown hair in bunches, sticking up like round Mickey Mouse ears above her head, and the same huge brown eyes as Jamie. She was dressed in a Newcastle football shirt, bright pink tights, and a pleated purple velvet skirt. Ashraf strongly suspected that someone was in the 'old enough to dress myself' stage. Said tornado launched from the kitchen doorway, and squealed with delight when Jamie caught her and whirled her around. She smushed their faces together in a thrilled hug, then beamed down at Ashraf and insisted on flopping forward to reach him.

"Hug!" she demanded, and Jamie laughingly handed her over. Ashraf ended up with a four-year-old standing on his thighs, hugging his head to her chest like her favourite football.

"Ashraf, this is Sammy. Sammy, this is my partner, Ashraf."

She let go and stared imperiously at him. "Are you an uncle or an auntie or an ankle?"

Ashraf had absolutely no idea why he would be an ankle. "Uh. An uncle, I suppose."

"Mummy!" she bellowed, and he felt his eardrums cringe. "Mummy, Mummy, I have a new uncle, I have a new uncle!"

She jumped right off his lap, landed on the tiles with a bone-shuddering bang, and tore off into the hall. Jamie laughed, then took her place, sitting down like they owned

Ashraf's lap and had only been temporarily relocated elsewhere. Ashraf wound his arms around Jamie's waist and kissed their neck.

"Ankle?"

"Sorry?"

"Why are you an ankle?"

"Oh." Jamie rolled their eyes. "She finally picked up on my pronouns last year, and Ellie tried to explain it by saying I wasn't an auntie or an uncle. So Sammy decided I was a mixture of both and calls me an ankle."

Ashraf snorted with laughter. "That's brilliant."

"It's pretty classic," Jamie agreed with a smile.

"Hello—oh, *hello*. Jamie, you absolute slag!"

The newcomer was definitely Jamie's sister. Ashraf had assumed that Jamie and their sisters all had different fathers, but he was plainly mistaken. Same eyes, same ears, same slim figure, even the original full bust that had given Jamie such issues. Ellie was, Ashraf decided, what Jamie would look like if they were a girl. She had long mousey brown hair in a loose ponytail, was effortlessly pretty with her no-makeup, T-shirt-and-jeans look, yet had the hint of someone distinctly not average: the very edge of what looked to be a large and elaborate tattoo was peeking out the edge of her top, like a black frill on the skin hiding under pink cotton.

"Hi." Ashraf held out a hand. "Ashraf Zaccaria."

"*Dr* Zaccaria, Google tells me."

Ashraf coughed. "Uh. Well. Yes."

"Very nice." She shifted the car seat from one elbow to the other and shook his hand. "Ellie Rice-Singer. That's my little girl who's adopted you already, and this is—"

"Gimme!" Jamie said, holding out their hands.

The baby that was produced from the car seat was tiny. It was only a few weeks old, still small and squashed in a white grow and clearly homemade matching woolly mittens and hat. It was very fair, and bright blue eyes peeked at its...well, ankle, Ashraf supposed, as Jamie cooed and cradled it to their chest.

"Hello, Pancake," they whispered, and Ellie sighed.

"Oh my God, *don't*, or you'll have Sammy doing it."

"Hell-*o*, my little itty-bitty Pancake," they said gleefully, and Ashraf snorted with laughter. "You wanna hold her?"

"Er, no thanks."

"Babies not your thing?" Ellie asked.

"Not really, no."

Still, he looped his arms comfortably around Jamie's waist and guided them to sit back on his lap with the baby. There, he could peer at her from a safe distance. She blinked sleepily at them both like a kitten, little noises escaping as Jamie took one of her mitten-clad hands and waved it gently.

"Aren't you *beautiful*," they whispered.

"Don't you want any?" Ellie asked as she set the car seat on the floor and took up her mum's empty chair.

"No," Ashraf said. "Never been interested in families." Or relationships. He tightened his grip, and Jamie smiled at him over their shoulder.

"Not very Italian of you," Mrs Singer commented as she blasted back into the kitchen with a laundry basket. "Jamie, you put that bairn back in her seat and get your shoes on. Sammy! Ellie, good God, get her coat."

Both Ellie and Jamie serenely ignored their mother. Ellie took her baby back, and Jamie rocked back into Ashraf to loop their arms around his neck and kiss his ear.

"Stop being so loved up, you tart!"

"Piss off," Jamie said, turning to stick their tongue out. "I snagged a good'un; let me enjoy him."

"You enjoy later," Mrs Singer tutted, snapping her fingers. "Dinner. Now. Get yourselves in the car—the children need to eat, and I have to exercise my rights as a mother."

Jamie scoffed. "What rights as a mother?"

She smirked—and then she looked *exactly* like Jamie.

"Questions," she said. "Now, *git*!"

Chapter Nine

ASHRAF HAD NEVER been to a Scottish christening before.

It was first thing on Sunday morning. The church was gloomy and cramped, nothing like the sweeping Italian churches he'd grown up with. The congregation was small and largely didn't seem to actually know Jamie's family. Ellie stood up at the front with the baby, alone, and when the water was plonked on her forehead, she dutifully howled like most babies at christenings, and that was that. Then they all went out for lunch.

Ashraf...didn't really see the point of it, truth be told.

Most of the people who came to lunch seemed to be Ellie's friends. They sat around gossiping, more than a few of them with babies of their own, and Ashraf found himself sitting back in a corner and watching Jamie entertain Sammy. He observed, trying to learn about Jamie via their surroundings, by the way they caught Sammy to twirl her around, or spent more time crawling around on the floor with the kids than chattering with the adults. He learned how they'd been brought up by the way their mum sat and drank, occasionally clipping a too-noisy kid around the ear yet was up in a flash and retrieving the granddaughter she'd supposedly been ignoring if Sammy went around the corner out of sight.

"You were a wild child," he accused when lunch finally arrived, and he managed to sneak Jamie back for himself for a little while.

"Me? Nope. Innocent. Wonderful. Angelic in every way."

Ashraf raised his eyebrows silently.

Jamie grinned. "All right, yeah, I wasn't the best. But Izzy was worse."

"Really?"

"Uh, yeah? Angry lesbian syndrome!"

"Don't you call your sister that!" their mother barked from the other end of the table, and Jamie stuck their tongue out in response.

"I wasn't too bad," they reiterated. "Just kept dying my hair and staying out at all hours. But Mam didn't mind too much because I was always out with this lad who was gay as a picnic basket, so I wasn't going to turn up pregnant, really."

"Well, some things never change," Ashraf said dryly, and Jamie cackled with laughter.

"What about you?" they asked. "Were you a problem child?"

"Think it depends who you ask," Ashraf said. "My father's so devout that his life's ambition was to meet the Pope and kiss his rings."

"Kiss his—sorry, *what*?"

"Not what it sounds like, you dirty—"

"Pope, Catholic, probably is," Jamie interrupted, and Ashraf rolled his eyes.

"Probably just as well you're not likely to meet my father any time soon."

Down the table, Mrs Singer narrowed her eyes.

"Not get on?" she asked bluntly.

Ashraf grimaced. "No. He, uh—"

He was about to explain about his father's faith, his anger when Ashraf returned to Islam, the history of bitter anger and grief between them after his mother had died—but then he remembered Jamie's words, and saw his chance.

"He's transphobic."

Mrs Singer's eyes narrowed further and flicked between himself and her youngest child. Then her face relaxed. The hardness bled out of it, and she smiled—really smiled, rather than offering a polite expression—at Ashraf for the first time all weekend.

Ashraf didn't realise how wound up he'd been until she smiled. But Jamie was right. It hadn't been his faith she'd been needling at all—simply his acceptance.

"He'd not really approve of Jamie," he told her, deciding to hammer the point home. "He barely grasps transgender people. Agender is about an entire staircase too far."

"I see," she said. "Wouldn't it be awkward? Never telling him?"

"Doubt it," Ashraf said, reaching for his glass of Coke. "He doesn't exactly approve of me either."

"Why not?"

He shrugged. "Gender. Sexuality. Take your pick."

And he left it at that.

JAMIE SHUT THE bedroom door and turned with a smile.

"So?" they whispered.

Ashraf dropped to sit on the bed, wincing at the creak.

"I think that went...all right, actually," he admitted.

Jamie had been right—his mum *was* nosy. Once he'd managed to drop the hint that he knew Jamie wasn't his girlfriend, she warmed up to him enormously—and immediately peppered him with questions. While they'd been often intrusive and somewhat rude, she also wasn't the slightest bit taken aback when he got short in return. She'd even laughed when he asked what his Egyptian mother had to do with anything, and complimented Jamie on finding someone who could handle them properly for once. The most exception she'd seemed to take all evening was his dislike of lamb.

"Told you," Jamie said and turned the lock on the door. They grinned.

"What's that look for?" Ashraf asked suspiciously.

"Mam likes you. Ellie thinks you're a looker. I happen to agree. And—" They rapped the door with their knuckles. "—we're locked in here. Just you and me."

"So, like every night back home."

"Just take your clothes off."

"Oh, you old romantic."

"Excuse me, *I'm* not heading for forty here."

"Rude."

Jamie rolled their eyes. They pushed off from the door and sat down abruptly in Ashraf's lap, throwing their weight into his chest and sending them both crashing back into the mattress. The bed groaned, and Ashraf echoed it.

"Shh, you big wuss."

"I'm wounded. I've been felled. Bury me before sunrise."

"Why? Allah have a time limit?"

"No, I just want to see you try and dig a whole grave in one night."

"Please." Jamie spread out over him luxuriously, stretching as if Ashraf—and not the sagging contraption under his back—was the mattress. "I'd just pop you in a bin bag and leave you out on the kerb for collection."

"Door-to-door funeral services?"

"Not paying for that. Landfill for you."

Ashraf dragged his arms around their waist and twisted them off to the side, rolling over to trap them.

"Dick," he said.

"That's yours," Jamie said, then beamed brightly and stretched up to dash their nose across the end of his own. "So, Mam likes you, Ellie thinks you're hot, and Sammy already thinks you're her uncle. Reckon I'm a keeper yet?"

Ashraf chuckled. "Already did."

"Yeah, but *now* you're stuck."

"That's you," he parried in a strange echo of Jamie's earlier remark. "And hey, even if they didn't like me, wouldn't bother me."

"I dunno...they're very good at reading people. It might have bothered me."

"Charming."

"Hey, trying to do better than my family record."

Ashraf pulled a face, sliding to the side when Jamie rolled their shoulder. They followed, cuddling into his chest.

"We ought to at least get undressed..."

"Mam doesn't turn the heating on at night."

"Oh." Ashraf reached down awkwardly for the duvet and hefted it up over the pair of them as Jamie resolutely refused to move. "Jamie?"

"Mm?"

"Thanks. For bringing me here."

"Shouldn't I be thanking you for coming along?"

"I guess, but this was kind of fun, actually. Well, not the christening. But lunch. Meeting your nieces. Your mum. Ellie."

"You'll like Izzy even more; she's big on history."

"Really?"

"Yeah. When I changed my name, she wound me up for months about not changing it to Indiana Jones. He was her idol when we were little kids."

Ashraf snorted with laughter. He lifted his arms over the covers, dropped them back around Jamie, and squashed them close.

"Ow!"

"Man up."

"Not a man."

"Woman up."

"Try again."

"Person up."

"Nope."

"Jamie up."

They chuckled and pressed a kiss to his neck.

"Deal. Now hug me to sleep. Got to be up early for that train back if you're going to make your first lecture."

ASHRAF WAS ALMOST glad for that first lecture.

Jamie's family were mad. Lovely, but utterly mad. Sammy was a whirlwind in a pink dress. The baby was, well, a baby. Noisy and demanding. Plus, Ashraf had heard of the insanity of a British Sunday lunch, but either it had always been undersold to him, or the Scottish version was infinitely worse. It had been a chaotic affair, crammed into that pub with all sorts of people coming and going—neighbours, friends, random supposed-aunts who bore no resemblance to anyone else—and a spread of food that was frankly ridiculous in volume for the small family actually in attendance.

They were lovely, but—overwhelming.

The sea of students staring back at him was actually welcome relief. And to make it even better, the lecture was about the exam topics. Mindless. Boring. He could switch off and relax. Just autopilot through it, and get his feet back under himself after his weekend.

But just as he was winding down, the door opened, and Callahan slipped in.

Ashraf's heart sank.

"Any questions, drop me a line as usual or attend my office hours," he finished numbly and nodded absently to the students to prompt them to pack up and go. He didn't take his eyes off Callahan, and they waited at opposite ends of the theatre.

Then Callahan nodded to the door, and Ashraf sighed.

An office talk it was.

He packed up in silence, already seething a little inside. He knew what this was going to be about. He shouldn't have shouted, shouldn't have let on to Kath that he knew about the complaint, should have let it alone, treated her with respect, and so on and so forth.

But Jamie had *cried*. They'd practically interrogated them in a meeting about their relationship. What was he supposed to do, just let that slide?

To his surprise, Callahan didn't steer him towards the department offices—instead, he made for a campus cafe. It wasn't one Ashraf particularly liked, but he didn't bother to complain. He simply took the offered cup, sat in the offered chair, and stared Callahan down.

"Ashraf—"

"I'm not going to apologise."

Callahan blew out his cheeks.

"You hauled Jamie into a meeting and asked inappropriately personal questions," Ashraf said. "They ended up in tears. What was I supposed to do, smile and pretend everything was fine?"

"I understand you're upset, but—"

"I want an office move."

"What?"

"I'm not working in that office anymore," Ashraf snapped. "She wouldn't have complained if I wasn't a Muslim—"

Callahan spluttered. "I—I'm sure that's nothing to do with—!"

"I don't believe you."

There it was. The more Ashraf thought about it, the more convinced he'd become. Kath had met Jamie. She knew the facts. And she'd complained anyway.

"Unless you can offer me proof that wasn't a factor," Ashraf said, "then I will continue to not believe you. Either she moves out of that office, or I do. I'm not working with someone who thinks that of me."

"I'm sure she—"

"Don't speak for her. If she wants to apologise, properly, she knows where to find me. Until then, I want nothing to do with her, and I don't want to hear anything more about it."

Callahan fell silent.

"You said yourself there's nothing in the complaint," Ashraf said. "So if this carries on, I'm taking it to HR. Or I quit."

He pushed his untouched coffee away, rose from the table, and walked away.

Chapter Ten

THAT SEEMED TO be the end of it.

He'd burned bridges, he knew. A week later, he got an email from Callahan with his new office number, and nothing else. Tom was quiet and awkward when he moved his things out. Kath didn't speak at all, buried in her work. He was quietly dropped from mailing lists and departmental events, and he found himself checking jobs boards and research postings as obsessively as he had when he'd reached the end of his PhD.

He didn't care.

Winter was rolling in. Jamie's trip—and their little jaunt—to Jordan was fast approaching, and they were typically either buried in their work or buried in their blankets on the sofa with a hot water bottle. Ashraf usually didn't run the heating until December, but Jamie struck a bargain—if he wanted to keep the heating bills down, the hug bill had to go up, and the kettle had to be boiling almost permanently. It was a good deal, and Ashraf took it.

Adjusting to sharing his living space took more out of him than he expected. And it wasn't the splitting of chores and bills that was the tricky part. Ashraf wasn't a naturally sociable person. He liked quiet company, liked researching or watching TV with someone, something that could be done in a companionable silence and quit without offence whenever he pleased. Jamie's effusive chattiness—even though they didn't seem to expect a reply—was difficult to get used to. Cuddling in front of the telly was easy enough, and sleeping together was a pleasant change, but the bubbly company in the morning and the conversation shouted through the closed bathroom door—that was a bit harder to cope with.

At least the confusing array of Jamie's stuff was amusing. He never knew if he'd catch them shaving their legs in the bathroom, or slapping aftershave on their neck for the more masculine smell. They would wash with flowery shower gels and bubble baths, then shake up a bottle of Right Guard or Lynx and cover the flowers with something that was advertised on the telly by a retired footballer, shot in vintage black-and-white to look posh and exclusive. And their shoe collection ran the full spectrum from steel-toe capped Timberlands to a pair of sparkly pink thigh-highs with a six-inch stiletto under each heel.

But he'd kind of expected all of that. The hardest adjustment was the bit he *hadn't* expected—that there was a downside to sleeping with Jamie at all.

Ashraf liked to cuddle. He even liked cuddling naked. All that intimacy, closeness, and warm skin—it was heaven. It was just the sex part that he had a distaste for, but as Jamie only seemed to wear clothes so as not to be arrested when they went out, he'd never felt any sexual pressure when cuddling with them anyway. Ashraf had just figured that Jamie's habit of going to bed in nothing but their birthday suit would just be an extension of those sofa cuddles he liked so much.

Not so much, as November proved.

The first Saturday in November, Ashraf was woken by Jamie burrowing their face against his armpit and mumbling something incoherent. He cracked open an eye, realised it was four in the morning, and grunted, lifting his arm to let them cuddle in and hoping they'd settle again in a minute. He *could* get up for prayer, but he didn't want to yet.

Then their leg was between his own, and fingers were scratching lightly through his chest hair. It was kind of nice. A damp kiss and a mumble were offered to his shoulder. A bit more intense of a cuddle than Ashraf was used to, and he was pretty sure Jamie was still asleep—but that was nice, too. Jamie still wanted to cuddle up, even fast asleep and talking to themself.

Then their hips rolled, their bare groin rubbing up his thigh and leaving a hot dampness.

He stiffened—and Jamie did it again. And again. A little rocking rhythm, like—

Ashraf's gut clenched tight. Just like that, all the happy haze evaporated out of his system. It was sex. Jamie was having a wet dream. Involving him. Involving having sex with him.

Ashraf had shot out of bed like he'd been scalded. The moment he closed the bathroom door, he felt ridiculous. Both for his reaction and for not expecting it. Of course, Jamie had wet dreams every now and then. What had Ashraf expected?

But that hot dampness, the sudden buck against him, the *intent* of it all—

He shivered. He didn't like sexual acts. And that had been unmistakeably sexual.

He'd not said anything, the first time. Or the second time, about a week later. But after the third, at the end of November, he found himself sitting back from morning prayer still turning the issue over in his mind.

And was still there when Jamie rolled over and threw a pillow at him.

"What y'doing?" they mumbled. "C'mere..."

"You didn't say you have wet dreams often."

Jamie blinked sleepily. Then frowned. "What?"

Ashraf sighed and heaved himself up onto the bed, but over the covers. Jamie looked drowsy and mussed, and he dipped in to kiss the side of their head, smelling sleep. "You've had a few wet dreams," he said quietly.

Jamie rubbed a hand over their eyes. "Yeah, and?"

And what?

Ashraf opened his mouth—but what was he supposed to say? Jamie was asleep when they happened. He knew full well if they'd been even remotely conscious, they'd take themself off to the bathroom like always. He couldn't blame them for something they'd done when they were unconscious. And anyway, it wasn't like they groped him or anything. They'd just tried to rub themself off on his thigh.

"Just didn't think you got those," Ashraf said lamely.

Jamie shrugged, yawning again. "Now and then." They stretched, lifting their back—and thereby the duvet still arranged over them—entirely off the mattress. "Breakfast? It's my turn, isn't it?"

"Um, in a sec. Thing is, it's..."

He trailed off. He wanted to say it. He'd never been in the habit of sidelining his sexuality in favour of anybody else's, and he wasn't about to start now. But what could he say?

"It's not your fault," he settled on eventually, "but it's...not something I like."

Jamie blinked. "Not—oh. *Oh.*" They sat up, combing both hands through their messy hair. "Hang on. I need to wake up. I'm having wet dreams on you?"

Ashraf coughed, feeling a heat rushing to his face. "You've...tried to rut my thigh a couple of times."

"That's all?"

He frowned. "It's still a sexual act, and I—"

"That's not what I mean," Jamie interrupted. "I mean, that's all I'm trying to do? Not kiss you or fondle you or anything?"

"No. You cuddle up to my side, and then you're... rocking."

"Thrusting?"

Ashraf cringed at the word.

"Probably because it's getting colder," Jamie said, yawning widely and barely covering their mouth in time. "I used to do it to my ex a lot. Morning sex almost every week during the winter."

"Great. So once a week for six months, I have to sleep on the sofa?"

"Probably not," Jamie said, leaning over to kiss his cheek. They looped their arms around his neck and sagged against him in a tired hug. "It's the nudity that sets it off, we figured out, me and Jack. I'll wear boxers or something."

"I can do that. You like sleeping—"

"No, it had to be me in the clothes."

"Ah."

"See? Easy." Jamie straightened up and nuzzled his beard. "Breakfast?"

Easy. Ashraf chuckled ruefully.

"Sorry. Still getting used to you being easy to negotiate with."

"Hey, long as you don't try and weasel your way out of cuddles. Then you'll hit the biggest brick wall you've ever seen."

"Deal."

THEY WENT TO Jordan on the tenth of December.

Professor Hanley had booked a hotel in the middle of Aqaba, on the Red Sea coast, that—judging by the Google search—was little more than a couple of rooms above a shop in a tiny narrow street. The point, Jamie had explained, wasn't a holiday—it was a diving trip with some students from an Australian university, and a couple of professors from a Jordanian university interested in exporting the artificial reef phenomenon.

That didn't change the fact that it was effectively a flat above a shop. Ashraf had taken one look and said, "It's your birthday. No chance."

Anyway, a week in a resort wasn't all that expensive, given he hadn't taken a holiday in about two years. So he went a little bit all out from his savings account and booked an all-inclusive stay at an adults-only resort down the coast from the town itself, with a regular shuttle bus service to get Jamie to and from their excursions with the others.

"You're mad," Jamie said when they saw the brochure.

"It's your birthday—and anyway, it's a holiday for me. I'm not sitting in a grubby little flat all day while you're off diving."

"You could come too."

"I can't dive."

"You could stay on the boat, though."

Ashraf shrugged, dispelling the unease that prickled under his skin at the very mention of it. "Not really my thing, thanks. I'm going to get a lot of my reading done."

"Just make sure it's some fun reading too, not just your boring old history books."

"They *are* fun."

Jamie had pulled a face that made their opinion of such things very clear, and it had all dissolved into a tickling match on the sofa.

Then the tenth arrived, and off they went.

Of course, there was no Newcastle to Aqaba flight. Tourists were overanxious about the Middle East, in Ashraf's opinion. He'd always meant to spend more time there—not only to learn about his mother's country, but also head east and explore the cradle of human civilisation—and then veer sharply west again, and compare it to the rich intrigue of Islamic Spain, the outpost of the Islamic world for centuries, and the most beautiful intertwining of European, Middle Eastern, and North African culture that he knew of. Since his undergraduate thesis, his academic interest was ancient man. Religion had seemed off-putting, and he'd wanted to avoid research bogged down with such matters—but Islamic Spain was the greatest challenge to that decision.

He'd just never gotten around to it. And, all right, he wouldn't get to do much in Jordan in just a week, especially with Jamie tied to the Red Sea, but he'd already booked them an excursion to Petra and Mount Nebo. If Jamie was going to get some fish, Ashraf would be damned if he wasn't going to get some history.

They got a short flight from Newcastle to London with Meg and George. Professor Hanley—despite his job— apparently hated flying and had insisted on minimising as much time in the air as possible, and would join them later on a shorter flight from Paris. As a result, George was surprisingly jovial. Ashraf had thought the man was incapable of smiling, but when they were both delayed for a so-called random security check, he joked with Ashraf the whole time they were having wands jabbed in their armpits and bags. He even managed to get the security staff looking vaguely embarrassed about their decision without being an arse and getting them both into trouble. Ashraf made a mental note to take lessons from him.

The layover in Heathrow was short, and all too soon, they were waiting at the boarding area for the flight to Amman, and Ashraf found himself closing his eyes and drinking in the sound of fluent Arabic all around him. Not the formal, beautiful intonations at the mosque, or the British-accented, slightly stilted Arabic spoken outside it just before and after prayers. Fluent Arabic. The Arabic he had grown up hearing at his mother's knee—albeit in entirely the wrong accent, and peppered with words he'd either never known or long since forgotten in all his years of speaking Arabic only to Allah, and not to other human beings.

"Hey." Jamie tugged his sleeve. "What are you doing?"

"Just listening."

A young woman with a Jordanian passport gave him a startled look.

"In English?" Jamie suggested.

"Sorry." He chuckled. "Just listening to the Arabic."

"Ah. Nice?"

"Very."

"You're going to teach me one day, right?"

"I don't know," Ashraf said. "I like it better when you're not butchering it."

Jamie rolled their eyes but didn't rise to the bait. "Oh, I checked with one of the guys who's taking us out on the water, and he recommended a mosque for Friday that welcomes visitors for prayer. He said you're welcome to go with him and his family while we're out there."

"Thank you," Ashraf said, reaching out to squeeze their hand. "I'll think about it." He liked mosque for the feel of it, but it wasn't necessary. Allah would hear him just fine from the hotel room on his usual mat.

"You know, I always assumed you were Christian, being Italian and all," George said as their seats were called and they got up and gathered their bags together again.

"I've dabbled in both," Ashraf admitted. "Christian father, Muslim mother."

"Christ, bet holidays were fun."

"Well, yeah, best of everything. Especially if Eid and Christmas lined up."

"Yeah, but what about when Ramadan and Christmas lined up?"

"Oh, yeah, that was pretty bad..."

They kept up the discussion all the way onto the plane, to the point where Jamie swapped seats with George and abandoned him to the chat. Being an avowed atheist, Jamie very notably didn't discuss religion at all with Ashraf, and they had a strict live-and-let-live policy. Ashraf found himself next to the young woman from Jordan and ended up chatting with her in Arabic, delighting in how the language eased from carefully thought out and enunciated, to flowing—as though he'd never spoken anything else—by the time the seatbelt signs came back on.

Amazing how, despite having never been to Jordan in his life, he felt at home when he stepped off the plane.

They drove from Amman to Aqaba. It was a long drive down most of the country, and it swept by in a surprisingly cool rush of sand and scrublands, tiny towns nestling by the main road, and dust swept up in great clouds by the trucks around them. Although the sky was clear, the season had ebbed to a pleasant warmth instead of the blisteringly hot temperatures it was famous for, and the air conditioning in George's hire car helped take the rest of the edge off. Ashraf sat up front and talked religion with George again, while the students in the back argued about—of all things—the misrepresentation of fish in Disney movies. He'd never met anyone who hated *Finding Nemo* as much as Jamie.

They reached Aqaba just before nightfall.

It was a surprisingly small town on the edge of the Red Sea—but they seemed to keep driving into it forever, the suburbs crowded with whitewashed houses and advertising billboards. On the horizon, great cargo ships in the port could be seen, and then George said he'd drop them off at their resort first, and the car swung out onto a coast road, following signs for Saudi Arabia.

And then Ashraf saw it. Water.

The first glimpse of the sea was between resorts and their half-built competitors. It shimmered off the shore, flat and bright under the sinking sun—and Ashraf's throat closed up. Sweat prickled on his skin. His heart began to beat harder in his chest. Car. Sea. In a car, by the sea. Following the coast road—

Blindly, he groped for Jamie's hand over his shoulder and dragged it into the crook of his neck in lieu of being able to hug.

It wasn't Mamma's car. It wasn't the Mediterranean Sea. It was a hire car, full of lively academic fish nerds, and they had every intention of going diving tomorrow.

It wasn't Terracina. It wasn't *then*.

"Hey, you okay?"

"Yeah," he mumbled. "Just tired."

"Me too, this morning was way too early..."

He closed his eyes. He'd thought he'd be fine. He'd thought it was just about getting in it. He didn't think just the sight of it would—would—

He was stupid.

Clenching up his face, Ashraf focused. He let Jamie's grumbling about airport arrival times consume him instead. Tyres on the rough road, Jamie's voice, the car radio chirping away in Arabic because George couldn't work out how to turn it off—not the sea. He couldn't hear the sea. It wasn't there. *It wasn't there.*

Slowly, Ashraf realised he might have made a terrible mistake.

Chapter Eleven

THEY HAD THE morning to themselves the next day.

Professor Hanley wasn't arriving—along with their Jordanian counterparts—until noon, which meant the others had elected for a lazy start. Ashraf got to wake slowly in a luxuriously big hotel room, with Jamie burrowed into his armpit and snoring lightly. He got to take the world's longest shower without worrying about the hot water running out, and then drip-dry while Jamie took their own, before donning light trousers and a polo shirt and heading down to breakfast hand in hand.

"I like this," Jamie said as they reached the breakfast bar. "Let's holiday every birthday."

"Might need to just do a camping trip for mine, given what this cost."

"I'll win the lottery or something; it's fine."

Ashraf laughed as they sat down—then stiffened.

Jamie had picked a table right by the plate glass windows that looked out over the hotel grounds towards the sea. He couldn't see the water itself through the cluster of straw umbrellas and the poolside bar, but he knew it was there all the same.

This had been a *terrible* idea.

"Okay," Jamie said, frowning at him over the table. "What's wrong?"

"I—what?"

"You went weird in the car last night as well, and now you're doing it again."

"Nothing's—"

"Don't pull that with me."

Ashraf bit his lip and tore his eyes away from the crowd of umbrellas.

"I've...not been near the sea for years."

"You *live* near the sea."

"Not within sight of it."

"You don't like the sea?"

"It can make me a bit nervous," he said. "It's fine, it's nothing. Just need to get used to it again."

"You sure?"

"Yeah. It'll be fine. By the time you get some free time, I'll be used to it again. I grew up near the sea, it's fine."

Jamie didn't look one hundred percent convinced but shrugged. "Okay," they said slowly. "Right, I'm getting some toast. Want some?"

"Yeah, sure."

They had a quiet breakfast, Jamie's excitement at finding pineapple juice hilarious given Ashraf could buy it in cartons at the corner shop down the road back home. He managed to get his mind off the sea, and by the time Jamie's phone lit up on the table with their summons from George, Ashraf felt as positive as he had on the plane. This would be fine. He'd grit his teeth and get over this nonsense about the sea—they had Jamie's birthday off to Petra and Mount Nebo away from the water entirely. He also had a Kindle crammed with research papers to get through and, as a reward, the latest Neil Gaiman.

This was going to be good, sea or no sea.

Jamie went off on the shuttle bus at half past twelve with a sports bag nearly as large as they were, crammed with their scuba gear, and Ashraf wandered back to the room to pick up his laptop and e-reader before deciding to find a sunny spot down by the pool. The lack of kids in the resort was a definite plus. He could get some work done, within waving distance of the bar and a steady supply of virgin cocktails, and maybe check out their sandwich selection and tide his stomach over until Jamie got back. He might have never come on a diving trip before, but he knew what Jamie was like after a training session down at the leisure centre. They could pack a surprising amount of food away for a five-foot-three piece of string.

The sun was pleasantly warm as he stepped out of the shadow of the building. He gave the pool a wide berth, but it wasn't in use and was little more than a shiny expanse of blue bracketed by bobbing plants. In the flowering season, it was probably beautiful. He could hear the trickle of a fountain somewhere. He picked a table without a shadow nearby and had barely lifted the laptop lid before a waiter appeared and took his order.

And then he heard it.

A hollow rustle, like wind through leaves only deeper. A crash. A sweeping sound of water scraping against sand.

Sea.

His fingers clenched tight on the edge of the table. His lungs were too small. He could hear a little girl screaming from twenty-six years ago, the sputter as a car engine cut out, the strange silence that seemed to echo in his ears before the water—

"Sir?"

He jumped violently, and the waiter took a step back.

"Are you all right, sir?"

The sound rubbed soothingly around his ears—and then the water crashed violently against on the shore, and Ashraf took a gulping breath.

"Yes," he answered in Arabic. "Yes. Thank you."

His fingers shook on the offered glass. He rummaged in his bag with his other hand for headphones. Jamie was always leaving their headphones in his things—and when his fingers closed around a pair, he felt tears burning alarmingly behind his eyes.

The music had never sounded so good.

A Disney soundtrack. It burst into his ears, bright and jovial, and cut off the sea with a happy hammer on the drums. He drained half the glass in one go. Even swallowing made him shake.

It wasn't there.

The sea wasn't there. It wasn't there. It wasn't.

And how could he have been so stupid? He might be an anthropologist now, but he'd been a historian from the very beginning. He knew the power of history. He knew the unshakeable force it exerted on the present, how it coloured every aspect of the world around them, how it commanded entire civilisations even as their own nature doomed them to repeat.

How could he have been so stupid as to believe that his own history could be so easily defeated?

HE STEPPED DOWN off the shuttle bus, and a breath of sharp relief rushed out of him when a familiar voice shouted from a restaurant on the corner.

He'd been summoned just as the sky had begun to glow gold from the impending sunset. It fell quickly this far south, and by the time the hotel shuttle bus had reached the middle of Aqaba itself, it was dark. But dark was good. Dark meant no water, and the jubilant music spilling out of windows and doors all along the road, belonging to both buildings and cars, meant no sound of the tide either.

He'd sat at that table for nearly five hours, blasting happy kids' music in both ears, and he'd barely read a word.

But Jamie's smile was a beacon of relief, and Ashraf gravitated towards it for a kiss before even acknowledging the others. Professor Hanley was nursing a large glass of something that smelled like it was four hundred proof, probably to recover from the flight. Their numbers had been boosted by four Australians and two Jordanians, one in traditional dress and the other in jeans and a brightly patterned headscarf that did next to nothing to hide her hair. She gave Ashraf a very obvious once-over, and he fought not to blush as he introduced himself.

"You study marine biology too?" she asked.

"Ah, no. I'm Jamie's partner. I'm just along for the ride."

"He studies anthropology," Jamie chimed in, and all but George scoffed as one. Ashraf rolled his eyes, used to it, and tapped the side of Professor Hanley's glass with his knuckles as he sat down.

"Another?"

"No, no, best not," Hanley said and squinted at Ashraf. "How are you doing, anyway? Not seen you since that nonsense with Callahan."

Ashraf grimaced. "Yes, that."

"Man's a twat," Hanley harrumphed. "Complete waste of time, that entire debacle. I don't know how they handle PhD students in *your* department, but mine have better things to do than sit in HR meetings."

Ashraf pulled a face but nodded at Hanley anyway. The man was shrewder than people gave him credit for. The typical haphazard professor when it came to anything regarding his job—the entire university knew George would be a shoe-in if he ever applied for a lecturer's position or a professorship, given he'd been doing Hanley's work single-handedly for years—Hanley was nevertheless sharp as a tack when it came to his own students. Could barely remember their names half the time, and Jamie had hammered their pronouns into his head by shouting them at the top of their lungs whenever he cocked them up, but he was famously tight about taking on PhD students. He insisted on interviewing all of them and could walk out of a five-minute chat knowing with one hundred percent certainty whether the student was a shirker or not. He'd been nothing short of a complete prick about Jamie's ex-boyfriend, Jack, who'd been a slacker and a major distraction, yet had been nothing but friendly towards Ashraf from the very first time Ashraf had shown up at the labs to meet Jamie for lunch.

"Thank you," Ashraf said.

"Eh?"

"For sticking up for Jamie in that meeting."

Hanley grunted. "Welcome, I suppose."

"One could argue you should have sided with Callahan. Student welfare and all that..."

"Student welfare would be a lot bloody better if we started treating them like adults, instead of wrapping them in cotton wool and pretending they're children. It's a university, not a high school."

Ashraf hummed. He wasn't so sure about that, especially when it came to the freshmen.

"Anyway, I saw the original complaint."

"You did?"

Hanley grunted as he knocked back another mouthful of the wallpaper stripper masquerading as alcohol in his glass. "Load of prejudiced bollocks."

"So it *was* prejudice?"

"Aye, though probably not what you're thinking."

"Oh?"

"Kept banging on about your age." Hanley squinted. "How old are you anyway? Thirty-three?"

"Thirty-five."

"Christ, to be thirty-five again..."

Jamie, who had been placidly listening at Ashraf's side, laughed at that. "Give over, Professor, you're only forty-one!"

"Shut your yap."

"Forty-one going on seventy," George said, and the sombre table of academics erupted into university students on holiday. Hanley called them all ungrateful bastards heading for fail grades on every paper between now and graduation, George started telling stories about a trip to the Pacific when he'd been a PhD student of Hanley's, and Meg and Jamie started swapping ideas for a seventieth birthday bash for the summer. Ashraf sat back and watched with a smirk, quietly resolving to never let his students ever find out either his age or when his birthday was. It seemed like an invitation to chaos.

Then Meg smacked Jamie on the arm and said, "You're having a romantic holiday with your boyfriend in the middle of a work trip! What you got planned, a moonlight dive? Skinny-dipping at midnight in the hotel pool?"

Ashraf's gut clenched. Sea. Swimming. No. He couldn't do it. He knew, with a savage certainty, that he just couldn't do it.

And if he couldn't swim—

"That just means I have better taste in blokes than you lot!"

"Better taste in blokes is an oxymoron," Hanley grumbled.

"Well, yeah, growing up in the nineteen fifties, you *would* think that..."

"Oi! Little shits!"

—then what was he doing dating a diver? If his own past still had him in that iron grip and could paralyse him with fear just from *hearing* the sea, then what the hell was he doing here, surrounded by fish nerds, sharing a bed with a person who lived and breathed water just as much as any mermaid?

What hope was there, if the very thing Jamie lived for was the thing Ashraf had nearly died in?

Chapter Twelve

"READY!"

Jamie bounced out of the bathroom in a see-through sarong and a string bikini, their intent on the hotel pool blindingly obvious, and Ashraf felt sick. Three days in Jordan had culminated here—Saturday at the hotel, to recover from gruelling dives yesterday and hours poring over the resultant photographs.

Tomorrow—their birthday, their twenty-fourth birthday—Ashraf was whisking them off for a long day trip at Petra, Wadi Rum, and Mount Nebo, but today was their lounging around the hotel day, their lazy day, and, being Jamie, they'd done exactly what Ashraf had feared.

Put their bikini on, found a clean towel, and set their sights firmly on the water.

Together.

"C'mon," Jamie said, slinging their bag over their shoulder and grabbing his hand. "Let's get one of those sunbeds right by the edge. I'm going to get you in the water and—"

"No."

It just fell out of his mouth. Jamie turned with a puzzled half smile.

"I didn't think you'd want to be right by the bar—"

"No, I mean—I can't go in the water."

"Why? Did you forget your trunks? You can just go in your shorts, you know."

"I can't."

"Maybe not *those* ones, they might chafe, but—"

"No," Ashraf interrupted. "I can't get in the water. At all."

Jamie paused.

Then, with a frown, they said, "What's wrong?"

Not, "why not." Not a laugh, and a yes, he could. That quiet, understated question. Ashraf's chest ached.

"I'm—"

Scared. Terrified. Paralysed by the very sight of the sea lapping on the shore. Breathless with fear at the sound of the water clapping shut over the heads of swimmers as they jumped into the hotel pool.

"I can't."

Slowly, Jamie backed him into the bed until he sat down with a thump. They sank down onto his knees, all warm skin and silky sarong.

"It's okay."

He slid his arms around their waist slowly.

"Whatever it is, it's fine," they said slowly. "How about you tell me what's wrong, and we see what we can do about it."

"There's nothing you can—"

"We can."

"—do about it."

"Well, what is it?"

Ashraf let out a shaky breath. "I can't go in the water."

"You can't swim?"

"No. Well, yes. But no."

"Um..."

"I know how to swim," he said tightly, "but I can't. I can't get in the water. I couldn't even—shit. Yesterday, when you were off diving, I tried to walk along the beach. I couldn't even step foot on the sand."

There was a long pause. Long fingers began to toy with his hair, combing a stray lock behind his ear and retrieving it when it only slipped free again, marginally too short to reach. The motion was familiar and soothing, and Ashraf closed his eyes.

"You're afraid of the water?"

The words were spiky and sharp, even though Jamie's tone was gentle. Ashraf felt his bones creaking under the pressure.

"Yes."

His voice shivered. But Jamie's was soft and firm.

"You have hydrophobia."

That—sounded better. It was ridiculous, but it did. Different word for the same thing, but Ashraf somehow preferred it.

"Yes."

"You didn't say."

"I didn't think it was this bad."

It had been years since he'd been near a body of water. He never went swimming, or into gyms or leisure centres where there might be pools. He didn't go hiking or rambling, so he never went down by rivers and lakes. England wasn't exactly famous for its beaches, so he'd never been to the coast in all these years of working and studying in the country.

When he cast his mind back, the last time he'd been near the sea—really *near*, like he was now—was when he was nine years old.

Twenty-six years.

"I haven't been near the water since Mamma died."

Jamie's fingers stilled. Their weight settled more heavily into him.

"You never told me what happened."

Ashraf swallowed. "She drowned."

"Oh. *Oh.* Oh, Ash—"

"She was ill. When my father left her, she stopped taking her medication. So her illness took hold again. Voices, paranoia, this feeling people were after her..."

"What people?"

"Any people. The government, my father, her family back in Egypt, you name it."

"So she—"

Jamie trailed off. Ashraf took a deep breath.

"She picked us all up from school in the car. She didn't usually. We always walked."

"We?"

"My sisters and me."

Jamie's voice dropped very low.

"I didn't know you had sisters."

"I don't now."

"Oh, God."

"She drove us round to my uncle's on the outskirts of Terracina. He wasn't in, so she put a letter through his door. When I was older, he told me it was pages and pages of paranoid ramblings. And at the end, she'd put that she wouldn't let them take us. Take me and my sisters. She'd not let them take her children away to be tortured."

"She thought someone was going to kidnap and kill her kids?"

"Her illness made her think it."

Jamie's arms slid around his neck, and their lips pressed to his temple.

"She drove—"

His throat closed up, and he buried his face in Jamie's neck. He could still hear it. His sisters screaming in the back. The water gurgling up the outside of the glass. His mother praying, just leaning against the steering wheel in tears and praying in a muddled mix of her learned Italian and her native Arabic.

He could still hear the sea as it slammed shut over the roof.

"She drove her car into the sea," he croaked, forcing every word out of numb lips, "with us in it."

Jamie breathed out in a long rush and squeezed him tightly.

"I'm sorry. God, I'm so sorry..."

She'd drowned. His sisters had drowned, trapped by the child locks in the back seat. He'd gotten halfway out and then the door had been forced closed on his leg.

And then he'd drowned too.

But he was the only one to wake up again. In a hospital, with a badly broken leg, and his grim-faced father at his side. The only one. He'd missed the funerals. Missed saying goodbye. Missed—for years, he'd missed—understanding how any of it could have happened.

"I knew I wouldn't be able to come diving, but I didn't think just *hearing* the sea would—"

"Okay." Jamie's voice was soothing. Their fingers began to comb through Ashraf's hair. "Okay, it's okay..."

Faintly, Ashraf realised he was crying.

"You don't have to get in the water," Jamie said quietly. "You don't ever have to get in the water if you don't wa—"

"I do."

"Why?"

Ashraf coughed wetly, pulling back to wipe at his eyes with his hands. Jamie stayed right there on his lap, their dark gaze trained unwaveringly on him.

"You're a diver," he said. "You love the water, you love the sea, it's who you are. I can't—I can't share your life if I can't even go near the thing you're most passionate about."

And there it was. The fear that surrounded the phobia itself. He was scared of the water—and he was scared of losing Jamie because of it.

"I wouldn't leave you because you can't dive with me, Ash..."

"Not deliberately," Ashraf croaked. "But—I can't go to the Seychelles with you. I can't go sailing with you. So you'd take your trips away without me, several times a year, and you'd talk about things I didn't see and people I never met, and eventually, we'd grow apart. Fall apart. And I don't want that. I want to be there; I want to share it. It's not fair if you come to digs and museums with me, and I wave you off at the airport with your scuba gear."

"I'm not...dirt-phobic," Jamie said carefully.

"It doesn't matter why it happens. The effect will be the same."

There was a long pause.

Then Jamie leaned back, cupped Ashraf's face in both hands, and smiled.

"You really think of this as permanent, don't you?"

Ashraf blinked.

"You and me," Jamie clarified gently. "We're not even a year old, and you're thinking like we'll always be here."

"Well...yeah."

Jamie laughed and nuzzled his cheek. It was such an emotional one-eighty that Ashraf found himself mentally fumbling for purchase.

"Love you too," they said. "Short-term, we can just stay out of the water."

"You like—"

"I'm also diving every day. Trust me, I'm getting my fix. Long-term, what do you want to do?"

Ashraf swallowed. "What do you mean?"

"Do you want to try and…recover, get past it somehow, or do we try and make this work with—"

"I can't."

"Can't what?"

Ashraf blew out his cheeks. "You know how I can't compromise on sex?"

"Yeah…"

"And how I said you can't go and sleep with other people either?"

"Uh-huh?"

"I can't compromise on *you*."

"What's that mean?"

"I mean, I want you. I want to be there all the time, even if it's just—you being you and fawning over fish and I'm just watching you be beautiful and you've no idea I'm even there. The more I miss that—the more I miss *out* on that—the harder it's going to be to let you go at all."

"Ah, I see."

"And if I start being jealous and possessive—"

"Then we'd fall apart anyway," Jamie finished, tugging on Ashraf's ear gently. "Do you think that's going to happen?"

"Eh?"

"Do you think you're going to turn into a possessive dick?"

"I—sort of?"

"What does that mean?"

Ashraf grimaced. "I can see me getting—annoyed, I guess? Getting antsy with not being there. But I know I'd just end it. I'd not try and stop you going."

"Well, if you tried to stop me doing my favourite things, then it'd be ended anyway, just not by you," Jamie said in a chirpy voice, then gently started scratching at his beard. "So, I guess we have a couple of long-term options, don't we?"

"Do we?"

"Yep. Either we work out a way that you don't feel left out when I go off on my diving trips, or we work out a way of getting you to join in a little bit."

"Diving? No chance."

A chuckle and a hug were produced in rapid succession.

"But maybe you could come out on the boat sometimes. Or swimming in the hotel pool. Or come to the Seychelles."

Ashraf swallowed.

"I can't even go and set foot on that beach out there," he said hoarsely.

"Maybe one day you can."

"How?"

"I don't know. Could look into some therapy. Maybe try and get you past the most extreme bits ourselves. You can always come to the pool with me when I go training." Jamie rubbed their hands briskly up his bare biceps. "How about for this week, we try something really, really small?"

"How small?"

"You walk out there with me, and we go sit at a nice table under that gazebo by the bar, and I get my cocktails, and you get to eat your body weight in fries like you did last night. Just us being us—all nice and straight-looking so there's no issues, and we can hear the sea and the pool, but we're not even close enough to get splashed. Yeah?"

His fingers were shaking. His throat was swollen and dry.

"I can't go on the sand," he whispered, hating himself for it.

"So we won't," Jamie said and slid off his lap. "C'mon. Bring one of your boring history books. I'll bring the laptop and type up my research notes for the day, and you'll make it ridiculously hard for me by constantly playing footsie with me under the table."

Ashraf managed a short laugh and got up from the bed. Book, drink, and—forget the conversation they'd just had.

At least for the moment.

Chapter Thirteen

JAMIE'S BIRTHDAY WAS a relief, in more ways than one.

The first was that Ashraf had booked an inland tour, where there was no water to be seen except that which was sold in bottles. Petra was an ancient city, lost in great chasms of unforgiving rock. Wadi Rum was a dry riverbed in the middle of the desert, where the silence was eerie and the idea of a tide nothing short of ridiculous. And Mount Nebo, where Moses had first seen the Promised Land, offered the barest glimpse of the Dead Sea, salty and still, in the distance.

No water. No pools. No sea. Nothing to be afraid of, in any sense of the word.

The second was that he'd lain awake most of the night worrying. Despite Jamie's assurances, Ashraf couldn't see much hope in the dead of night, with the sound of the sea beyond the window keeping him constantly twitching, the dreams of his mother putting her foot down on the accelerator as the sea rushed up to meet them playing over and over in his head, and his tired, anxious mind picking apart their relationship and watching it unravel like a film. But then he took them to the must-see sights of Jordan, and their face lit up when they smiled at him like he was the centre of the universe.

It undid the whole sleepless night.

He wasn't prone to bouts of insecurity—thanks to a mixture of his aromanticism and his pride, he suspected—

but it had crept in a little last night all the same. Cutting Jamie off from sex was one thing, but that was something that could be done. Cutting them off from the water was impossible, and Ashraf had contemplated whether it was worth trying if his phobia was this strong.

But then Jamie beamed at him and threw their arms around his neck for a cheesy romantic selfie in the narrowest part of the passage down to Petra—the rose-coloured rock shadowing them in the tight chasm, and Jamie's joy crushed in against Ashraf's cheek like they were nothing more than newly-weds on holiday—and...his worries eased.

He was being daft. They'd talked about everything else. Jamie wore pyjama bottoms in bed and jerked it in the bathroom when they needed some sexual relief because they wanted him more than they wanted sex. Why get himself wound up that they couldn't figure out a workaround for this? Jamie was right. He didn't need to go diving with them—he just had to be able to smile at them from the deck of the boats they jumped off, and cuddle them in their wetsuit and damp towels when they surfaced again, babbling excitedly about barracudas and barnacles, brighter than a kid at Christmas.

And it helped that while Jamie moaned about his history obsession, they weren't entirely immune to the wonders of ancient ruins. They insisted on going to the monastery above Petra, high on the mountainside, despite the several million steps in unyielding sunshine to get there, and peppered him with questions about the peoples who would have lived and worshipped here, the religions they would have followed, and how an entire city could have been lost in the first place.

At the top of that mountain, Ashraf slid his arms around their sweaty waist and towed them close for a kiss.

"Happy birthday," he said, pressing their noses together and closing his eyes. "I love you."

With their smile twisting the intimate little cocoon of their faces, he was gifted another soft kiss.

"Love you too," Jamie whispered. "Thank you for coming. For bringing me here."

"Thank you for asking."

Arms looped around his neck comfortably.

"We can sort this out, you know."

"Yeah?"

"Mm. We're sorting everything else. Why not this one?"

Ashraf laughed. "I guess so."

"I know we shouldn't work," Jamie continued. "Muslim, atheist. Historian, scientist. Bookworm, thrill seeker. You're teetotal, I still go out and get absolutely blotto every month with the LGBT society. No interest in any kind of politics at all, while I go to protests and parades every summer. Ace, allo. Twelve-year age gap. Italian-Egyptian, Scottish for about six million generations. Hell, we can't even say we're a gay *or* a straight couple."

Ashraf chuckled. "Guess you're right."

"It doesn't matter," Jamie said. "I love you. I feel like I'm the most amazing person I can possibly be when I'm with you. You're good for me—and I'm good for you too. We *do* work, even if we shouldn't. So it might take a bit of hard work to maintain that if you're afraid of the water, but—so what? We can do it."

Ashraf swallowed thickly, wound both hands into the hair at the nape of their neck—and kissed them.

It was a hungry kiss. A desperate kiss. But it was also a certain kiss. He knew this person, he knew this soul, and he knew just how Jamie fitted around the edges in his own psyche, how he smoothed out the edges in theirs, until—

joined together—they created something perfectly smooth and uninterrupted.

So he kissed like his soul depended on it, even though there was no need to be afraid of this.

And when he broke for air, he didn't release a single lock of hair, and whispered, "I *love* you," so close that he could feel the words rather than hear them.

Jamie squeezed tightly, rumpling his own hair, and smiled against his mouth.

Then—because they were Jamie, incorrigible and ridiculous, and those being two of their better qualities—the smile widened into a broad, mischievous grin, and they bit his lower lip before pulling away.

"You are never going to be able to top this birthday. You've screwed yourself there."

Ashraf laughed, catching their hand before they could escape, and towed them back towards the steps.

"Hanley's right, you *are* a little shit," he said. "Come on. Let's get some tourist tat and then try a donkey ride back up to the visitor's centre. Got to be done, doesn't it?"

"Donkey?" Jamie said and snorted. "Maybe for you, old man. *I'm* going to try a camel."

Ashraf squeezed their hand, both of them sweaty from the climb and humming a bit. Despite the sea, despite the fear, despite everything saying that he ought to just sit back and let the end come—he had never felt better.

JAMIE WENT DIVING again in the morning.

They skipped out on breakfast to head into the centre of Aqaba and meet the others, so Ashraf spent a leisurely morning with his book on the balcony. But as lunchtime rolled around, he set it down on the table and stared out over the road. Their view wasn't exactly glamorous—a dusty construction site opposite, clearly for a rival hotel chain by the glossy billboard advertisement that almost shielded the shell from view—but it beat the sea.

And with that thought, he tucked another book into his bag and slung it over his shoulder.

He'd not realised how bad it had become. He used to like the sea when he was a kid. It was the only time his parents ever got along, a family day out at the beach. He'd learned to swim in the sea, splashing around in armbands while his sisters made fun of him for not knowing how yet. He'd been the smuggest six-year-old in the world when he finally got the hang of it and spent every weekend until he was nine years old in or around the water.

He'd loved the water, once. And Jamie loved it now.

Leaving the hotel room was easy enough. It wasn't until he reached the bar where he'd sat the day before that the sound of the sea reached his ears and he stopped dead, in the middle of the walkway.

It wasn't loud. Just the gentle rush and fall of water. It sounded calm. He could see glimpses of blue between the straw umbrellas on the beach, but nothing else. Yet even the sound of it had sweat breaking out on his forehead and his fingers clenching tight around the strap of his bag. He felt sick.

"Come on," he told himself firmly. "First sunbed on the beach. First one."

The beach was deep. The sand at the edge of the path was thick and dry. The sea hadn't been all the way up here in forever. The weather was still. If he just sat on the nearest sunbed, he'd be completely out of reach. Could read his book, listen to the sea, and nothing could happen. Nothing at all.

"Nothing can happen," he said to himself.

He didn't move, though.

"Nothing can happen."

Nothing *did* happen.

"You are thirty-five years old," he said through gritted teeth. "Do it."

Jamie would be back by five. They would come looking when he wasn't in the hotel room. They'd find him here, on the beach. Progress already. Hope. If he could just do this one thing, then there was hope. If he could do this part, then he could do all the other parts in time. Jamie would know it meant he was trying. And they were patient. If he were trying, they'd wait forever for him to get there.

But—

He turned around and headed back up the path to the bar.

Chapter Fourteen

"HEY!"

Arms slid around Ashraf's shoulders, a kiss hit his cheek, and then Jamie was past him, stealing a mouthful of his virgin cocktail.

"Mm, nice," they said and sat down in the other chair. "Good day? Hungry yet? I'm starving; I think I must have swum the length of the Channel."

"Yes, yes, and I doubt it," Ashraf said, marking his place and closing the book. "Good day?"

"Bit boring to be honest," Jamie said. "It's no fun diving when you don't get to enjoy the view. D'you want to eat here or go into town and find somewhere?"

"Here's good."

"Ready now or—"

"I tried to go on the beach," Ashraf interrupted.

Jamie raised their eyebrows. "Yeah?"

"Tried."

"Tried's good."

"Didn't manage it."

"You still tried," Jamie said, shrugging. "What stopped you?"

"Seeing and hearing the sea?" Ashraf said tartly.

Jamie laughed. "Well, okay, we get one of those white noise machines at home, and I'll play the tide every night while you sleep. And we'll get a huge painting of the sea and hang in on the wall."

Ashraf rolled his eyes.

"It'll work!" Jamie enthused. "How about tomorrow you try something else?"

"Like what?"

"Like tomorrow when I get back, we sit at the bar itself, not one of these tables."

Ashraf glanced over at the bar. "So?"

"Ten feet closer to the pool."

Ashraf blinked—then laughed. "Should have known better than to try discussing this when you're hungry."

"Yes, yes you should."

Still, Jamie's presence was buoying. Just like it had been on the mountain, their effusive affection was soothing. He had all the time in the world and a partner who would support him every step of the way. What was he worrying about? There was no deadline on it.

They ate at one of the resort restaurants. They were going home the day after tomorrow, and Ashraf had every intention of eating his fill where he didn't have to check if the meat was halal or hunt for vegetarian options to avoid the pork. Jamie granted his wish by trying every single one of the local dishes on the buffet, liking only two or three of them, and foisting the rest off onto him.

"You have to make me some of this," they said about the bean dip, though, and Ashraf laughed.

"You can buy that at the Asian supermarket near the mosque."

"Then buy me it, whatever, I just need more!"

"I'll make you a deal," Ashraf said. "If you stop buying jars of Ragu, I will introduce you to good Egyptian food."

"What's wrong with Ragu?"

"It's swill. It's offensive. My stepmother would have you crucified for even touching the stuff."

"She's a snob then; it's lovely."

"You're a philistine who's clearly never had proper Italian food."

"Because you won't make it!" Jamie protested. "You never do!"

"You never ask."

They both bitched and moaned throughout the meal, a warm contentment settling over Ashraf's mind as the sky darkened outside and the restaurant slowly filled with other couples similarly flirting. On a whim, he took Jamie's hand once they were done and pulled them to their feet, towing them towards the doors that led out to the poolside.

"What, skinny-dipping?" Jamie laughed.

"You should be so lucky."

"I *should*."

"No. I just—figured that I ought to be bold."

"Eh?"

"Like you."

"Bold like me?"

"Yeah."

"So you *are* skinny-dipping?"

Ashraf pulled a face as he reached the end of the walkway, where the beach met the resort, and stopped.

Stopped there, with his toes just barely over the edge of the gardens.

Jamie waited at his side, silent and patient. The sea waited beyond the sand, rumbling and roaring in the twilight. Right there. Gurgling. Like it had rushed up the windows of the—

Ashraf stepped forward—and stumbled.

Like the wind had been knocked out of him, he stumbled. He staggered blindly for a sunbed, groping like it was pitch-black, and sank shakily down onto its padded cover with a grateful lurch in his stomach. The sand squished coolly into his sandals—and then there was a warmth in his lap as Jamie sank down onto him and pressed him back onto the bed.

Their mouth was hot on his own, and their hands firm over his ears.

He closed his eyes and listened to their pulse. Warm. Strong. Grounding. He was fine here, in their arms. Jamie wouldn't let anything happen, even if it could. He was perfectly safe and eternally supported.

Ashraf slid his arms around their back and surrendered.

THE MINUTE THEY landed at Heathrow, Jamie's phone started buzzing.

"That'll be Mam," they said. "She's still mad we're going for Christmas so late."

"Hence the next flight?"

"Hence the next flight."

Their connecting flight wasn't back to Newcastle, but Edinburgh. They were staying at Jamie's mum's house for Christmas, under her orders. It was also an hour later than the London to Newcastle flight, and Ashraf took the opportunity to stretch his legs. Jamie—who could find even aeroplane seats roomy—stayed curled up with their bags across a couple of seats in the departure area, and Ashraf abandoned them there in favour of exploring. The first stop was a decent-sized drink instead of a tiny can, and a proper hot meal instead of the contents of a lukewarm foil box. He firmly maintained it was permissible in Islam to eat pork on a plane because it wasn't real meat anyway.

After that, Ashraf's pit stop at airports was always the tech section of the duty-free. He never underestimated the need for a good power adaptor or a decent set of headphones. And he liked to play with his tech before he bought it, not just look at a picture on Amazon like Jamie did and take a chance.

Still didn't appreciate the uncomfortable looks from the clerk as he examined the goods, though. The airport at Amman had been such a pleasant break from the usual airport crap he had to put up with that the side-eye and awkward coughing grated even more than usual.

And then he saw it—and forgot all about the cashier.

It was just a little black box sitting on a shelf, no bigger than the kitchen radio at home. Mains power supply with a battery backup, and a headphone jack under the volume control. And the little leaflet promised not only a range of preprogrammed tracks but the ability to add his own if he plugged a USB stick into the back with the right files on it.

A white noise machine.

Jamie had made the remark flippantly in Aqaba, but suddenly, it seemed like a good idea. The ocean was one of the preprogrammed tracks, according to the label. And if he could learn to associate the noise with nice things—like snuggling on Sunday mornings with Jamie when it was cold outside—then maybe it would take the edge off the sea a bit. Maybe he could sit on those sunbeds furthest from the water next time.

And if not, he could switch on the rain track and give Sunday mornings that extra dose of smugness anyway.

He bought it and headed back to Jamie with a determined spring in his step. They were carefully playing a game on their phone, their tongue sticking out in concentration, and looked both ridiculous and pretty at the same time. Ashraf didn't want to lose them. He didn't want to lose this. And if twenty pounds for a white noise machine would help him get over his phobia, then he'd buy a new one every week.

"Look," he said, wedging himself into the chair behind Jamie. They grumbled and flopped back into his lap, lifting the phone above their face to continue playing. "Hey. Look."

"In a minute…"

He took the phone away and replaced it with the white noise machine. The look he got told him that Jamie was seriously considering beating him to death with said machine.

"What's this?" they asked in a tone of voice usually reserved for finding maggots in the kitchen.

"A white noise machine."

They raised their eyebrows.

"You suggested it, and I found it. It plays the sea. I can listen to it at night, and train myself to like the noise instead of being afraid of it."

The venomous look eased somewhat. Jamie turned the machine over in their hands as if inspecting it but looked to Ashraf instead.

"You think it'll work?"

"Can't hurt to try."

"Until you have panic attacks or nightmares at home."

Ashraf winced. "Okay, it *could* hurt. A bit. But it could also really help. Bed with you is one of my favourite places."

Jamie cooed, then grinned and said, "Anyone else, that would be a pass."

Pulling a face, Ashraf tossed an arm over Jamie's stomach and grazed their ribs lightly with his nails in a warning tickle.

"Don't you dare."

He smirked and then bent double for a kiss. Jamie nudged their nose against his own affectionately as he pulled back, and smiled.

"If it gives you nightmares, I'm switching it off," they said. "But you're welcome to try it."

"If it gives me nightmares, maybe we'll just have to play it during the day for a while first."

"Yeah, maybe. Does this mean I get extra cuddles at home?"

"If I give you extra, I'll never get to work or prayers, and you'll never get to go swimming."

"I see no problem with that," came the lofty reply.

Ashraf smiled and began to finger-comb Jamie's hair.

"Tell you what," he suggested. "I'll try it tonight at your mum's place. Then if I have a nightmare, you'll be practically on top of me, thanks to that tiny little bed."

"Deal," Jamie said and held up both hands in a cup shape. "Now give me back my phone."

Chapter Fifteen

THEY DIDN'T GET to bed until very late.

Ellie came to collect them from the airport, with both Sammy and Baby Pancake wedged into the back of her car. Jamie ended up crushed between the car seat and their exuberant niece, and Ashraf quietly sent up a quick prayer of thanks for being given the front seat. Then he took it back when Ellie delivered them to a carvery restaurant, overflowing with noisy Scottish ankle-biters and very little in the way of halal or vegetarian options, and proceeded to bend his ear for nearly three hours about having children.

"I *can't* have children," he eventually had to fall back on, which was both technically true and not the reason why at all, and then Jamie ruined the potential sombre get-out-of-questioning-free card by sniggering madly.

"He *hates* kids," they said when Ellie shot them a look. "'Can't' has nothing to do with it."

"So—you can?"

"No."

"Can't *and* won't," Jamie said, hefting a clamouring Sammy onto their lap. "Never underestimate Ashraf's 'won't.' *What*, sweetie?"

They didn't find respite at Jamie's mum's house either. She had brews ready and was in a towering temper about them not arriving until today. It was a time for family, she insisted, and family meant here—and apparently, here by the fifteenth at least. Jamie then took exception to what—

for them—had been a study trip being boiled down into 'gallivanting off in the Middle East' and Ashraf had beaten a hasty retreat to the squashed little living room on the pretence of finding and petting Mrs Singer's scrawny black cat.

By the time they actually got to bed, he was considering just skipping the night entirely and restarting with Fajr again.

"Sorry about that," Jamie said as they closed the bedroom door and began to unceremoniously strip down to their underwear. "Ellie said she was in a right mood about the trip."

"If it was going to be that much of a problem…"

"It's not really, she's just sulking," Jamie said tartly as they crawled onto the bed. They twisted over to sit cross-legged against the pillow, naked but for their boxers. "I usually come up right after term ends, and the last boyfriend I had wasn't the bring-him-home-for-Christmas type anyway, so I think she's struggling to get used to it."

"Don't your sisters bring men home?"

"Izzy's gay, remember?" Jamie said. "And Ellie's not had one for ages."

"Huh," Ashraf said, leisurely changing into his pyjamas and fishing in his bag for the white noise machine. "I'd have thought with three kids, she'd be used to other halves."

Jamie shrugged. "Not so much. She'll like it by tomorrow. More people around."

"She like a busy Christmas, your mum?"

"Likes a busy life," Jamie corrected. "She's still grumpy she only had three kids."

Ashraf wrinkled his nose. "Urgh. Three kids. Who voluntarily has three kids?"

Jamie laughed, budging up enough to let Ashraf slide into the bed, then promptly taking up residence on top of him like an extra blanket.

"Izzy arrives tomorrow," they said. "I don't know if she's bringing her girlfriend or not. There's a mosque about two miles away if you want to go to Friday prayers—I already asked Ellie, and she said you can borrow her car if you want..."

Ashraf hummed as he set up the machine on the bedside table. When he switched it on, the gentle sound of a breeze through autumn leaves filled the little room.

"That's nice," Jamie said, situating themself firmly over his chest and sighing gustily. "Night."

Ashraf hovered his thumb over the button to change the track. The next one would be the ocean. He took a deep breath and looped his free arm over Jamie's shoulders.

"Here goes nothing," he murmured.

And pressed.

THE SUN WAS up by the time he woke.

Blinking groggily, it took longer than usual for his brain to come online. Friday. Quiet. A watery sun gleaming in a cold blue sky. The aftertaste of a terrible nut roast on his tongue. Blergh.

The clock said ten past nine, but he felt shattered. Jamie was nowhere to be seen, and Ashraf levered himself out of the bed and rummaged for his prayer mat. First things first. It had been nearly fifteen years since he'd started a day without morning prayers and—late or not—he wasn't about to start now.

Still, he wasn't so devout as to think Allah was all that particular about the actual time—it was predawn somewhere, after all—so that sense of peace settled back over him all the same. Whatever life could throw at him, he could deal with it. Sea or no sea.

The house was silent, and he slipped from bedroom to bathroom undisturbed. He showered quickly, the water chilly and the room even more so, and took his time warming up in the towel by carefully seeing to his beard. His scalp hair was wild enough at the best of times, but his beard could get frizzier than a pubic thatch if he didn't watch out.

By the time he was dressed and ready to investigate where his partner had gone, sound had started to give away Jamie's—or at least someone's—position downstairs in the kitchen. Ashraf plastered a polite smile on his face as he headed downstairs, but dropped it in favour of a kiss and a cuddle at the sink when he found Jamie alone, washing breakfast pots and humming to the radio.

"Oh! Hello."

"Hi." He squeezed. "You didn't wake me for prayers."

Jamie gave him a funny look over their shoulder. "You were awake for prayers."

"I was?"

"Yeah. You barely slept more than an hour at a time."

Ashraf pulled back, blinking. "I did?"

"You don't remember?"

"No."

Jamie huffed. "You just kept waking up, constantly. Mumbling at me in Italian. I think, anyway, it didn't sound like Arabic."

"Nightmares?"

"No idea. I mean, you were a bit clingy, but you weren't screaming or crying or anything. And you'd drop back off again if you got a bit of a cuddle out of it. I turned the machine off at something like three in the morning, but it didn't seem to help."

"I do feel exhausted," Ashraf admitted. "I don't remember dreaming though."

"Well, maybe you'll get used to it. Hey, you want to go out and get breakfast? Mam's taken the kids to the park, and Ellie's gone to pick up Izzy from the train station. We could nip out and have the morning to ourselves. Get a better blanket for the end of that bed."

"You just want to buy another fleece."

"I also want to get five minutes to have a proper hug without a small child trying to wedge herself into it." Jamie dried off their hands before turning on Ashraf and kissing him. "Mm, get this," they added, stroking his beard and tugging lightly. "C'mon. Let's get the bus into town and have a bit of a wander around. I know a sandwich shop that serves a whole roast dinner in a roll."

"That sounds disgusting," Ashraf said, but rubbed his nose against Jamie's ear and kissed the lobe. "We'll negotiate on the food."

It was freezing outside. Jamie was pink before they'd reached the end of the road, and their beanie got progressively lower and lower around their ears and neck. When they shoved their hand in Ashraf's pocket at the bus stop, he couldn't help but laugh.

"It's cold!" they whined. "I want to go back to Jordan."

"Next Christmas, I'll take you to Italy."

"Will it be hot in Italy?"

"Not roasting, but not double-underwear weather either."

"Deal."

"How are you not used to this?" Ashraf asked as the bus pulled up. "You're Scottish."

"And you're half-Egyptian, didn't mean you were wandering around in jeans and a jumper in Aqaba," Jamie groused as they boarded.

"Touché."

The ride into the city centre was nicer than the one out when they'd visited for the christening. It was quieter, and people were less interested in them. Ashraf relaxed back against the seat, rubbing his tired eyes with one hand and keeping the other affectionately tucked around Jamie's waist. Despite the cold, he felt warm. At ease. So the white noise machine had seemingly caused a nightmare or two, but—despite the exhaustion—he didn't feel worse off for it. He could deal with that. Maybe over the next couple of nights, he'd settle and sleep properly again.

Jamie insisted on buying the new blanket before breakfast, so Ashraf was starving by the time he was allowed to finally pick a cafe and drag Jamie inside. Eggs on toast had never tasted so good, and nursing a coffee while Jamie tore their way through a fry-up was made infinitely better by the way their hair popped up, fluffy and wild, when the heat finally permeated their cold Scottish soul and rendered the beanie too warm.

He did get stabbed in the hand with a fork for the cold Scottish soul comment, though.

"So," Jamie said once they'd inhaled three-quarters of their breakfast. "The white noise machine is a bust."

"It's not."

"Either it's a bust, or you're sleeping on the sofa when we get home."

Ashraf laughed. "Give it a week. If neither of us can get a decent night after a week, I'll try it in the evening instead."

"Fine," Jamie grumbled. "What's next after that?"

"Eh?"

"Listening to the sound of the sea doesn't mean you're going to be able to come diving next summer in Australia with me," they said.

"To be totally honest, I don't think I'll ever be able to go diving," Ashraf admitted.

"Okay. So, how far do you want to go?"

Ashraf blew upwards into his hair. "I don't know. Far enough I can share it with you."

"Far enough to get on a boat, maybe?"

Ashraf chewed on his lip, then nodded.

"Okay," Jamie said. "So that's the end goal, get you to a point where you can get on a small boat without a problem. How d'you reckon we can get there?"

"I've no idea."

"Maybe thera—"

"I'm not going to therapy."

Ashraf hated therapy. He'd had to sit through endless tedious sessions of it all the way through his undergraduate program, and had hated every last minute of it. Three years of various counsellors and psychiatrists to somehow prove he was a man before he was allowed to actually transition and make his body look the part—which had amounted to three years of them attempting, more or less, to prove him wrong. If it hadn't been his love of supposedly feminine things like cuddles and poetry proving him to be a woman after all, it had been his sexuality as a symptom of his dysphoria rather than just an ordinary, boring old sexual orientation like any other.

Frankly, he'd rather walk off a pier into the North Sea than walk into a psychiatrist's office.

"I'm not doing it," he said tightly. "I've had enough of so-called experts prattling on that they know me better than I do."

"Okay," Jamie said gently, reaching to squeeze his hand on the tabletop. "Sorry. Didn't realise that was a no-go area."

"Well it is," he snapped.

Jamie raised their eyebrows, and he grimaced.

"Sorry. Shouldn't have snapped."

"No, you shouldn't," they said pointedly. "But if you're that anti-therapy, it probably wouldn't help anyway. We'll park that idea for the moment."

For good, more like.

"We'll think of something," Jamie said and stretched back in their seat. "In the meantime—ready for Christmas with our mad lot?"

Ashraf smirked and set down his empty cup.

"Bring it on."

Chapter Sixteen

IZZY, JAMIE'S ELDEST sister, was exactly what Ashraf had expected. Jamie had always described her as a mad army lesbian, and that was exactly what barrelled through the door—a short woman with short hair in a brutal buzz cut, wearing combat trousers and a hideously ugly Christmas jumper. She was built like a car, squat and wide—and then she squealed like a six-year-old and swooped down on Jamie in a hug.

"Jam sandwich!" she shrieked. "It's been too long, look at your hair, and who's *this*!"

Ashraf offered a hand, but got a hug, too.

"Ashraf," he squeaked over her shoulder, and she cackled with laughter in his ear.

"So I've heard!" She drew back and thumped him in the shoulder. "Ellie tells me you're Jamie's little addition to the family?"

"Guess so."

She grinned. She broached the gap between Jamie and their mother, Ashraf decided. She had the same bulky build as Mrs Singer, but Jamie's oddly monochromatic colouring. She had the same light brown—or dark blonde, depending on the season—hair, and the same impossibly dark eyes, set off by the same very fair skin that could burn or freckle, depending how sudden the sun and how careful the owner.

"Not brought a newcomer of your own?" Jamie asked as they heard the front door close.

"Nobody to bring this time," Izzy said brightly, slinging herself down onto the battered armchair in the corner. "Ellie! Get us a brew!"

"Make it yourself, you lazy slag!"

"Fuck off!"

In an instant, the friendly brick of an older sister turned into the drill sergeant. Ashraf swore he felt his eardrums cringe at the explosive volume of her curse.

"You be grateful Mam isn't here..."

"You can fuck off too; I can take Mam."

"Big words for a pussy!"

"*I'll* get the brews," Ashraf said, levering himself up off the sofa with a laugh. He fended off Jamie's protests and passed Ellie in the doorway to shuffle into the cosy little kitchen. He heard the shrill laughter of his partner and their sisters over his shoulder and smiled to himself as he filled the kettle and switched it on. Rummaging noisily for cups and spoons, he decided he'd just have to assume that all three took their tea the same way.

He and Jamie were the same in that regard—Ashraf had had two older sisters once, too. He imagined it had been very similar. The fighting over shared toys, the competing for attention, the heinous wars over such silly things like ice cream flavours and Saturday morning cartoons—and then the unity against parental schemes to withhold snacks, to administer punishments, to enforce homework rules and bedtimes. He remembered them all crawling into bed together to hide when their parents fought bitterly. He remembered the night his father walked out, not for the row and the smashing plates and hearing Mamma lose her Italian entirely and screaming at him in furious Arabic—but for the warmth of the blankets over his head, his sisters' hair scratching his face.

His sisters were gone. But he wondered, now, if things would have changed. If they wouldn't send him abusive WhatsApp messages from Terracina. If they would accept him and Jamie, the way his father couldn't. If they'd be married, have kids, be gay like Izzy, be trans like him. Maybe he'd had a brother, and he'd never known.

Yet Ashraf couldn't be down, not with the background noise of Jamie shouting at their sisters in the next room, and Izzy's crowing laugh. He found a tray and inched carefully back into the living room with the mugs, to find them all crowded together on the sofa and going through Jamie's phone, a picture of his own house just visible on the screen.

"Here you go," he said, distributing the mugs on the coffee table. He then shamelessly hauled Jamie up by the armpits, twirled them around in front of him, and sat in their vacated spot, dragging them back down into his lap. They laughed and flopped back against him, putting their bare feet up onto the coffee table.

"You're disgusting," Ellie said with a chuckle.

"I have better taste than you, excuse me for being proud," Jamie scoffed.

"All the shit I got when I brought Grace last Christmas!"

"Because you wouldn't stop necking with her, it was revolting!"

Ashraf smirked into the back of Jamie's shoulder—and then it was turning, digging into his chest, and there was a hand under his chin.

Then he was kissed.

And yes, he knew Jamie was making a point. He knew the kiss was nothing more than show for their sisters—he just didn't care.

He cupped the back of Jamie's neck and kissed them back.

"MAMMA!"

He lurched upside. A weight slid off him. Someone shouted—maybe him, maybe her, maybe—

"Ash!"

Breathe.

This—

He closed his eyes and pressed the heels of both hands into his face. A sudden silence deafened him. Then dry, warm hands covered his own, and lips touched his temple.

"It's okay. It's okay. Shh, it's okay. There's no water. No sea. You're right here with me. It's okay..."

The silence was the white noise machine, Ashraf realised. Jamie had switched it off. He breathed out in a long, ragged rush, and reached out blindly for it.

"Ash, *no—*"

He switched it on, and before the first swell of water could reach his ears, clicked it through to the next track. The sound of rain filled the little bedroom, and Jamie's arms slid right around his neck and drew him into warmth and their familiar smell.

"It's okay," they whispered. "It's all right..."

"Shit," he croaked.

He'd not dreamed about it in years. *Decades.* The grief and loss had been debilitating, but in the sense that he slept like the dead, for fourteen hours a day, for years. In the sense that he lost all energy to live, never mind to dream. The few nightmares he'd had when he finally emerged on the other side of that horrific collision of bereavement, trauma, and identity, had been about normal things. Things that seemed pathetic in comparison to what he'd already been through.

But never that. Never her. Never them.

So, once he could breathe again—nose pressed to Jamie's shoulder, the drumming of rain in his ears—he wasn't sure what he was supposed to do. Get up and pray? Try to go back to sleep? Have a cup of tea?

"What now?"

"Sorry?" Jamie murmured.

"What do I do?"

"What do you mean?"

"What do people do after nightmares?"

Jamie laughed gently. "Oh, sweetheart. Okay. C'mon. Let me make a big fuss of you, that's what you do now."

He allowed them to get him out of bed and stripped from his sweat-soaked pyjamas into a pair of warm jogging bottoms and a spare T-shirt. Then they both snuck downstairs. Izzy was sleeping on the sofa, the living room door firmly closed, but Jamie took him into the kitchen by the hand. They sat in Ashraf's lap at the table, force-feeding him tea and biscuits, before slowly finger-combing his hair back into place.

"Thanks," Ashraf mumbled in the end, resting his head into the crook of Jamie's elbow. "I guess we have to try the machine during the day instead of at night for a while."

"Guess so," Jamie murmured.

"Sorry I woke you."

"It's fine. Hazards of the whole partner thing."

Ashraf smiled faintly, closing his eyes at the soothing sensation of being petted.

"Just be patient," Jamie said, kissing his hairline softly. "We're here for a nice Christmas. My sisters like you. You've convinced Mam you're a keeper. I've decided on a nice romantic New Year kiss at Edinburgh Castle to see the fireworks. And then we can start on all of this next year. Deal?"

"Yeah," Ashraf whispered. "Deal."

Chapter Seventeen

ASHRAF THOUGHT JAMIE forgot about it.

They had their planned joyful Christmas, which was nothing like Italian Christmases he'd had growing up, or—thankfully—the nauseatingly cheesy Christmases he saw on the telly. It had been a huge mess of presents, screaming sort-of in-laws, and a lot of enthusiastic kisses under various plants, mistletoe or otherwise. And then they had welcomed in the new year with a kiss at midnight, freezing everything but their lips off, in the middle of a crowd of cheering Scots at the firework show in Edinburgh. A kaleidoscope of explosive beauty bursting overhead, and he'd ignored the lot of it.

They got back to the post-Christmas rush. He remembered it from being a PhD student himself: the moment the supervisors suddenly remembered they had students at all and started demanding outlines and literature reviews and research plans left, right, and centre. Suddenly, Ashraf was left to his lectures and his library books, and Jamie was a silent ghost at the end of the sofa, their pale face made paler by the laptop screen, and working through the coffee Ashraf faithfully provided in silence.

It was nice. Peaceful. *Domestic.* Ashraf was finding that he rather liked domestic.

So it came as a rude shock when he was roused on a Saturday morning, about four weeks after their return from Jordan, to a kiss and a swimming kit.

"Come on," Jamie said. "You're coming to the gym with me."

Ashraf frowned. "I don't do gyms," he said heavily, with the same weight as not doing maggots or group sex in car parks.

"I'm going swimming," Jamie said, "and you can watch, and then we can sit in the sauna or the spa pool afterwards."

Ashraf bit his lip. "Jamie…"

"You don't have to get in any water that you don't want."

He exhaled heavily through his nose. "I couldn't even wade in the Red Sea."

"And if you can't get in the pool, that's fine. We'll go in the sauna."

"People will stare."

"They won't," Jamie said promptly. "I've got all my training gear. You can sit on the side and time me, and nobody will think twice. Promise."

"Promise?" His voice sounded feeble, even to himself.

Jamie leaned down and kissed his cheek. "Promise," they whispered. "Shane comes all the time and pretends to be my training partner so he can use the sauna on my membership."

A sauna *did* sound nice…

"Fine," Ashraf said. "But I'm not getting in the water."

He'd never been to Jamie's gym. Ashraf just wasn't a gym-goer—he privately thought of them all as stuffed with arrogant posers admiring themselves in the mirrors, and failed dieters pretending their fifteen-minute stroll on a treadmill was going to burn off their five doughnuts at lunch. But Jamie's gym was more of a health spa than anything else, with an Olympic-sized swimming pool bracketed on both sides by small hydrotherapy pools, steam rooms, and saunas.

They took the Metro. It was icy out, a slushy rain drifting out of a steel-grey sky. Jamie was chatty and effusive, taking Ashraf's hand on the train and refusing to let go all the way there. They were wearing fingerless gloves, and Ashraf stroked the cool nails one by one in quiet fascination, admiring the gleam of glittery silver nail polish against the stark wintry world.

"Can't we just stay here?" he asked plaintively when Jamie stood up for their stop.

"Nope. C'mon." Jamie tugged. "Don't you want to see me wet?"

An old lady looked startled, and Ashraf chuckled. He rolled his eyes as he was led off the train through the bustle, and out onto the main road.

"You did that on purpose."

"I did, but it's also true," Jamie admitted.

"Maybe. Could see you wet in the shower, though."

"Not swimming."

"What's the difference?"

"All muscle and motion. Trust me," Jamie said, "you're going to like this."

Ashraf wasn't so sure.

The lobby smelled like pool. He didn't mind that, really. Even kind of liked the clean, fresh smell. They had to part ways at the changing room doors, and he distracted himself by being as obnoxiously laddish as possible, stripping off like he was allergic to cotton and loitering with everything hanging out for a good few minutes.

And then he put his trunks on.

And stopped.

Ashraf hadn't been swimming since he was nine years old. He hadn't so much as waded. He *could* swim—he'd been very good at it, once—and it was a bit like riding a bike, he'd been told. And Jamie had told him thousands of times that the pool didn't have a deep end. It was one metre thirty, all the way across. He could walk in it; the water wouldn't even come up to his shoulders.

But he just stood there.

He didn't want to do this.

He curled his fingers around his towel, ready to call it off. There was a cafe upstairs. The windows overlooked the water. He could go and watch Jamie train, and then buy them an apology for chickening out. Jamie wouldn't even be mad. They'd understand.

Ashraf swallowed...and brought the towel to his chest.

"It's not the sea," he told himself.

It wasn't the sea. It didn't roar and swell and crash. It was shallow and calm. It smelled of chlorine and had edges and a flat bottom. He didn't even have to get in. He could take Jamie's stopwatch, and sit with his legs over the side, and time them.

Ashraf squared his shoulders and headed for the poolside.

Every step was like wading through...well, water. His feet felt flat and clumsy. His chest was tight. The echo of sound beyond the archway was hollow. Like the shouting above the surface, when—

He stepped out into the pool area—and breathed.

The pool was a flat disc of blue. Bright blue. No waves, no tide, no crashing foam. He could see the stripes on the tiled floor, and the lane dividers lay motionless on the surface. Jamie was standing on the edge in a sleek red costume, fitting goggles and a cap into place. They waved, smiling, and Ashraf managed to smile back.

"I can't get in," he said the moment he was close enough to whisper it, and Jamie squeezed his arm.

"That's okay," they said. "My bag is just there. Stopwatch and notepad."

"What do I write down?"

"The times of every length, and which stroke. Just copy what Shane's done. I'm going to warm up."

They dropped into the water like they belonged there, a lithe length slipping under the smooth surface. They slid along, nearly motionless and silent, and broke the surface a third of the way down the pool. Ripples flocked outward, the water gently bubbling as temporary hills formed but refused to break.

Ashraf slid down to sit cross-legged on the side and watched in fascination.

The hotel pool had been turbulent and chaotic, like an uncontrollable sea. Here, Jamie was the only life underwater at all. They looked alien, with the cap and goggles, yet so beautifully human all at once. Long, sleek limbs flowed with the water like they were one of their beloved fish. Their shoulders and hips were no longer joints, but soft sweeps under skin. Their spine flexed with both power and grace as they turned, feet punching into the wall, and they came flying back along the bottom, the water once again closed and calm over their head.

Slowly, Ashraf opened the notebook. It was only a quarter full, all neat tables and times in messy handwriting. Ashraf flicked to a random page three-quarters of the way in and began to write lightly with the pen. Carefully. His fingers were still used to Arabic, although mainly so he could take notes on his students during seminars without them sneaking peeks, and the whorls and curves of the lines remained familiar, even if he had to think before he spoke these days and some words had slipped away.

But these words hadn't, because they belonged to Jamie.

He stole a glance as Jamie powered into the third lap. Jamie loved the water. If they could breathe it, they would. They'd put off university for a year to learn to dive first, and they'd been to the Seychelles five times, but never to Spain. They were studying fish. *Fish.* They were going to have a doctorate in *fish.*

Ashraf eyed the water dubiously.

If he couldn't overcome this, then what future would there be? He'd never be able to go to the Seychelles. He'd been left behind at the resort in Aqaba all day, every day. What would be the point in going at all? There was no way he could ask Jamie to give it up—nor would he want to—but...

The water flicked above Jamie's heels as they turned and came back down the pool, a frog under the rippling surface.

Ashraf took a deep breath, clenching his fingers around the notebook and the single sentence in Arabic he'd written there.

And slid his feet into the water.

The cold kiss was a shock. It had been so long it almost felt slimy. Close. A wet grip, almost hard, around his shins.

But it didn't pull. It hugged but didn't tug. His feet drifted weightlessly beneath him, and the tiles were hard under the seat of his trunks.

When Jamie arrived, their hands came up either side of Ashraf's knees, and their chin landed squarely on the left cap.

They *beamed.*

"Ready?"

Ashraf wiggled the pen and mustered up a tentative smile.

"Ready."

WHEN ASHRAF FINALLY emerged from the changing rooms, Jamie was waiting in the lobby with two large cardboard cups.

"A reward," they said brightly and rocked up on the balls of their feet to deliver a kiss before delivering the cup. Ashraf smiled and took a sip. Hot chocolate. He raised his eyebrows in surprise, and Jamie beamed. "Thought indulging your sweet tooth might persuade you to come with me next week too."

"The sauna might have done that."

It hadn't been quite as good as watching Jamie lounging on the balcony in their bikini at the resort in Aqaba, but it was a close second. They'd been alone, too, so Ashraf had held Jamie's feet in his lap and stroked the soles gently, watching that pretty face dissolve into bliss.

So he slid an arm around their waist, hooking them close for another kiss, and smiled at the surprised squeak that escaped.

"No kidding," Jamie said but nudged free again. "C'mon. Let's brave the cold and go home. I really do have to start ordering my books in for my thesis."

"Proactive of you."

"We-ell..."

Ashraf raised his eyebrows. "Oh, right. What's the plan?"

Jamie blew upwards into the stray bits of hair escaping from their hat. "Professor Hanley wants Meg and me to go back to Australia with him next summer and start working on actually establishing a new reef."

"So?"

"So I have to get the theory done *soon*, like…by Easter soon, so we and the team out there can start on the logistics of the thing. Then we fit our new baby reef with cameras to monitor what life takes interest and film it—obviously, the Australian team will have to take charge of actually—"

"Jamie. Not into fish. English."

Jamie pulled a face. "That *was* English."

"Sure. Cut to why your baby reef means you're starting your thesis before you've even finished the first year. You should be on research and data collection still, surely?"

"But we can't start data collection until we have a semi-successful reef structure in place."

It clicked. "Ah. So you need to know what everyone else says works to make that happen, and see if it does work."

"Yes!" Jamie's face lit up again. "And reefs take time. I mean, we won't even know by the end of the PhD if it's worked. I'm hoping to get a research position to continue—maybe even in Australia itself, who knows, and—"

Ashraf caught himself mentally calculating whether he could do his own research from Australia, and quashed it.

"—it means that my thesis will only have indications of it working rather than conclusive proof, which means it has to work *well*, so—"

"Okay!" Ashraf interrupted, throwing up his hands. "Okay, okay. I get it. Fish magic has to happen so you can get a distinction."

"Least fish can swim," Jamie said snottily. "Your apes had to go the long way around."

"They did not—there's every evidence that prehistoric man was—"

Jamie smirked. Ashraf groaned.

"I walked right into that."

"You did."

He slung an arm around Jamie's shoulders. "That was low."

"Aw, you know I love you best when you're a dork," Jamie cooed and stretched up to kiss his cheek. That flush of warmth in Ashraf's face at the contact was echoed in his stomach. "But you can't exactly accuse me of nerdery. Pot."

"Kettle."

Jamie stayed under his arm all the way to the Metro station, and when the train came, it was packed enough that they hung onto Ashraf, who hung onto a support strap. He looked down and beamed, knowing full well that the pair of them probably looked ridiculously loved up. But Ashraf didn't care. He had someone brilliant literally holding onto him with both hands—why would he not smile?

And he'd put his feet in the water.

All right, he'd backed out of getting in. That was a bit too much. But he'd sat on the edge, put his feet in the water, and stayed there for a hundred lengths. He'd not had a panic attack like he had in Jordan. He'd even enjoyed earning himself a wet kiss when Jamie dragged their soaked body back out, water streaming off their perfect skin.

"I might have enjoyed that," Ashraf admitted quietly, and Jamie smiled, butting their forehead lightly against his neck.

"We'll make a swimmer of you yet."

Ashraf grimaced. "Don't get your hopes up."

"You *can* swim, can't you?"

"Probably. That's not the point, though."

Jamie cocked their head. "What is the point?"

"I told you," he said. "I can't share your life if I'm terrified of water."

"And I told you, I don't entirely agree. It might be harder, but I think we can work with harder. We work with hard already."

Ashraf smiled humourlessly.

"That might be interpreted as sexual by dirtier minds than mine," he said.

"Oh please. I've seen you sniggering at Swear Trek on Twitter."

As the train spat them out at their stop, Jamie's chilly fingers slid between Ashraf's own and squeezed.

"How about a reward," they said. "You came swimming with me. Want me to come and do something historical with you?"

Ashraf squeezed back, then let go and slid an arm around Jamie's waist instead. "I have a better idea."

"Yeah?"

"You, me, fleece blanket, TV."

Chapter Eighteen

"THIS IS THE biggest load of pseudo-scientific bullshit I've ever seen."

Ashraf grinned at the indignant tone and reached for another bit of popcorn.

They were both completely naked under Jamie's blue fleece. It was an enormous fluffy blanket that could have covered the sofa twice over, and it cocooned them both in soft warmth. Jamie was lying between Ashraf's legs, their head laid back against his chest, and one of their hands stroking his bare kneecap idly even as their voice had been one indignant rant from the first five minutes.

"I can't believe you've never seen *Stargate.*"

"It can't be popular," Jamie said.

"There's like...ten seasons. And two spin-off shows. And a film—though technically the film came first, so—"

"Oh my *God.*"

Ashraf laughed, tucking his nose into the crook of Jamie's neck.

"Why do *you* like it?" Jamie demanded. "What, this Mongolian tribe have just magically kept the exact same culture for nine hundred years? I don't think so! And why does it look like Canada? It looks like Canada."

"We can always watch something else."

"No, I want to see how they try and explain that—that *thing* in that guy's guts."

Ashraf stroked his hands down bare arms, back up to rub down a naked chest, and settled them on Jamie's stomach. He curled his fingers against soft skin and tucked his nose back into his favourite spot to breathe in the faint scent of Jamie's shower gel.

"Stop distracting me."

Ashraf flicked a nipple. "Not distracting you."

"Bloody aces," Jamie grumbled and caught Ashraf's fingers in their own. They wound them all together, joined fists of skin and sinew, and rested the lump against their belly. "There. Cuddle and let me watch."

"Thought it was bullshit."

"It *is* bullshit," Jamie said petulantly, and Ashraf chuckled. He wriggled a thumb loose so he could stroke it gently over the thin skin above gently rising ribs, nudging the soft swell of a small breast with the edge of his nail before returning along the same path when the breath was released and the ribs fell once more.

This was what he wanted now, he realised. He'd never asked for it, never wanted it before, never missed it—but now he had it, he wanted to keep hold of it forever. Listening to Jamie's outraged denial of the more outlandish concepts of a science fiction show. The heady, sensual touch of skin on skin, with the peace of nothing yet to come. The absent-minded stroke of toes against his ankle, and the tickle of hair at his neck. The smell of homemade minestrone lingering in the air, and the bowls stacked up inside each other on the coffee table. Even the soft gurgles and swishes of the fancy fish in their tank, the water ripples dancing on the ceiling.

"This is perfect," he murmured.

"Look, I'll grant you, that romance subplot with the colonel and—"

"Not the TV show! You and me. *This.* This is perfect."

Jamie laughed. "What, me shouting at your TV is perfect?"

"As long as you don't start insulting *Ancient Aliens*, then yes."

"Ex*cuse* me? You *watch* that?"

"I'm an anthropologist; of course I watch it."

"That's like me watching *The Little Mermaid* and calling it a documentary!"

"I didn't say I *believe* it," Ashraf griped. "I said I watched it. It's funny!"

Jamie slapped his knee, then turned over and propped their chin on his chest. He wriggled lower to ease out the uncomfortable-looking arch their spine had to perform to do it.

"Even if you never manage to come to sea with me," they said, "I still think this is the best thing that ever happened to me."

"Yeah?"

"Well, second-best."

Ashraf raised his eyebrows. "What comes first?"

"Finding that cafe with the triple chocolate cake of doom."

He laughed. "Okay, yeah, I'll give you that. You're my second-best find too."

"You didn't find me, I found you."

"Same difference."

"Is not. You didn't have a clue I existed before I kissed you at that bus stop."

"Er." He couldn't argue with that. He hadn't even known Jamie's name. "That's true."

Jamie pulled themself up to straddle his naked hips and slid their arms around his shoulders. He tweaked their bare nipple teasingly as the blanket slid down, then tucked it back around them both.

"I wanted to ask…" Jamie started to say.

"Yeah?"

"About your family."

Ashraf winced. "Ah."

"I don't—I don't mind not having met them yet," Jamie said carefully, "but on the proviso it's a temporary situation."

"How d'you mean?"

"You've spent Christmas with mine, and I've never even seen yours. I'm not even really clear on who there is to see, to be honest. I mean, would I meet your dad, or your aunt and uncle?"

Ashraf blew out his cheeks. "Okay. Well—my father and my stepmother live in Terracina still. But I haven't seen either of them in years, face-to-face. We just exchange cards now and then. Sometimes Chiara rings for a catch-up, but not very often. My father prefers to pretend I don't exist."

"What? Why?"

"Because I'm the last living reminder of the mistake he made in his twenties," Ashraf said. "He married my mother because he got her pregnant with my oldest sister. They'd been going out maybe two months, and then suddenly they were married and within a year had a baby and another on the way."

Jamie winced. "That—doesn't sound like it went well."

"It was awful; they hated each other. Mamma was a devout Muslim; my father was a devout Christian…"

"Sounds fun."

"Yeah. He walked out when I was nine."

"Nine."

"Yeah."

"The same year your mam…"

"Yeah."

"Oh, sweetie—"

"He left her for Chiara," Ashraf said bluntly, running over the incident with determination. "After—after Mamma died, I went to live with them, but it was strained. He didn't want me there, and...honestly, for years, I held him responsible for her death. The way he treated her killed her, in my mind. I went to live with my aunt and uncle in Napoli when I was fourteen, and I came to the UK when I was twenty-one and never went back."

"So..."

"I suppose my equivalent of meeting your mam would be taking you to Napoli."

"What about your cousins?"

"We're not close," Ashraf said. "We could get married, and I'd not invite most of them to the wedding."

"So there's not really anyone *to* meet, is there?"

"Not anymore," Ashraf said. "If we'd meet ten years ago, it would have been Nonna."

"Nonna?"

"Nana."

"Oh!"

"She'd have liked you. Me, not so much, but she'd have liked you."

Jamie laughed. "Me? Why?"

"Enthusiasm," he said. "She was always—*happy*. Insisted on it. Said life was too short to be miserable. Not that she knew anything about life being short, she was in her nineties before she died."

"Oh, good, I get to keep you for a good long time," Jamie said, twisting sideways and settling back into his side. "I suppose that's a trade. You can't meet my grandma."

"No?"

"Nope. She's in prison."

Ashraf blinked. "Your *grandmother*. Is in *prison*."

"Yep."

"Why?"

"Stabbed her neighbour with a meat cleaver."

"Wow."

"Mam's mam. Never knew my dad's mam and never wanted to. Or either of my granddads. Mam's auntie is Granny, really, but she's got dementia now and she gets really upset when she sees me."

Ashraf frowned. "Is this the one we didn't go and see at Christmas?"

"Yeah. She can't tell if I'm a boy or a girl anymore," Jamie said quietly. "And she's fine if she thinks you're someone else, but she thinks I'm two people at once, and that's when she realises she's losing her mind and gets upset. So I can't go anymore. I write her letters and Mam takes them to read to her. She thinks I'm the one in the army, that's why I don't visit. It's kinder this way."

"Oh, hell, I'm sorry..."

"It's okay." Jamie shrugged under his arm. "I guess we both kind of suck at families."

"Little bit."

"Disney syndrome."

"Eh?"

"Dead mums everywhere."

Ashraf laughed. "Doesn't that make me the princess?"

"You're more of a princess than me."

"*How*?" he asked incredulously. "You had a boob job, I had a bit more than that!"

"*I* don't use a whole bottle of hair conditioner in a week," came the snotty reply. The sombre tone of the conversation broke, and Ashraf dragged them back between his legs to trap them in a four-limbed hold and start tickling.

The scream in his ear was definitely Disney princess levels, but the savage bite to his jugular when he said so was less Belle and more Beast.

When they both eventually resettled—on the floor, the blankets and half the cushions on top of them, and the fish looking disgruntled at the chaos—Jamie wriggled up to kiss his ear, his beard, and his mouth in quick succession.

"Take me to Terracina and show me where you grew up, even if your family is a bit off limits," they said softly, "and we'll call it even."

"Deal."

Chapter Nineteen

A NEW ROUTINE emerged on Wednesday afternoons.

It was the afternoon off at the university, when Ashraf had no lectures and Jamie had no classes. So after grabbing lunch together on the campus, they would get the Metro up to the leisure centre, and Jamie would train while Ashraf— tried.

Some days were harder than others. The white noise machine didn't give him nightmares anymore and was even pleasant to wake up to in the mornings, but it wasn't making the pool any easier. The sounds were all different, and while he liked the clean smell, that was the *only* thing he liked.

So some days, he could sit on the side like that first time, knee-deep in the water and writing love notes in Arabic on random pages around timing laps and counting strokes. Some days, that was easy. And some days—like the fourth week they tried it, in early March—he had a panic attack in the changing rooms and had to get dressed again and head to the cafe that overlooked the pool to wait for Jamie to be done.

He'd been furious with himself, but Jamie's patient calm had soothed it.

"You're doing great with the noise machine," they said. "And given you nearly fainted when you went on the beach at Aqaba, I'm really proud of you for getting near the pool at all. Don't stress yourself out too much."

Easier said than done.

On the seventh week—in mid-March—he managed to slide into the pool proper and stand at the end waiting for Jamie to return. His heart had been threatening to beat out of his own chest, and then his reward had been Jamie sliding right up to him, that wide smile lighting up their features, and pressing every inch of themself against him in a deep, wet kiss.

"Getting there," they whispered, intimately close, and Ashraf smiled, tugging on a tiny curl of fair hair that had escaped from their cap.

"What do I get when I get there?"

"Anything you want."

What he got was a reward after every session. It was shameless, obvious psychology, and Ashraf didn't care. From long spells in the sauna to let the heat soak right into his bones and watch Jamie sprawl out in their swimming costume, to getting his favourite takeaway on the way home and feasting on the sofa under Jamie's blankets—Jamie bribed him, and Ashraf unashamedly let them.

At the end of March, he managed to tread water while waiting for Jamie, hands within inches of the side wall and shoulders artificially high in the water, but it had been a form of swimming anyway. Jamie had nearly exploded with delight, giving him another intense poolside kiss that had almost gotten them kicked out—and that was how Ashraf found himself drying his still-damp hair as he sat on the side of the bed, waiting for Jamie to come out of the bathroom.

"You didn't tell me what you wanted for your reward!" they shouted through the locked door.

Ashraf dropped the towel into the hamper and sat back on the bed, pondering. What he *really* wanted was Jamie not to go out tonight. They had a party to go to. But Ashraf wanted them to stay home, with him. He had a low burn in his chest and a keen need to put on a film and completely ignore it in favour of a takeaway from round the corner and the most intense snuggle of his life. Get Jamie's warmth and smooth skin completely intertwined with his own, and *be*.

It was the closest thing to arousal he ever got, and he wanted to indulge it and get a little kissing done. But the occasion was Tabitha's gender reveal party—the first time she'd be going out as *Tabitha*, instead of Dan, and the first time most of her friends would see her as she really was— and Ashraf couldn't begrudge her that. She'd been building up to it for nearly a year and was completely terrified. She needed Jamie there, and all the support she could get.

He just—really wanted that snuggle session, too.

"Oi! Did you hear me?"

The neighbours banged on the wall. Ashraf chuckled when Jamie banged back.

"I heard you," he called. "I'm thinking."

The bathroom door cracked open and a flood of steam gushed out. Jamie emerged naked, a towel pinned in place around their head. They crawled, damp, over Ashraf's prone form and sat proudly astride his hips, tall and beautiful.

"Think faster," they commanded, rubbing the towel in brisk motions.

Ashraf reared up, kissing each nipple reverently as he rose until he could slide both arms around that hot, damp back and bury his face into their neck to kiss a lazy pulse.

"Can I get a rain check on my reward?" he asked the pulse. "I know what reward I want, but I have to be in the mood."

"Ooh, I like." Jamie bit his ear. "Why not come with me, then?"

Ashraf wrinkled his nose, still tracking his hands up and down Jamie's back. He usually hated going to parties. He didn't drink and everything was just too loud, too hot, and too—well, sexual seemed like an odd complaint to have with Jamie in his lap like that, but...*sexual*. Casually sexual, instead of intimately sexual. Sexual, not sensual.

"C'mon," Jamie coaxed, nuzzling his ear. "Come dancing with me. The others would love to see you, Tabby would really appreciate your show of support, and then, when I'm a drunken mess, you can steer me safely home."

"No, you're all right," Ashraf said, patting their bum. "You can get a taxi. A load of drunk people doesn't sound like much fun."

Jamie pouted, then slid off his lap. They bounced over to the dresser to start rummaging—and the towel slipped.

"What is *that?"*

Jamie beamed and ruffled up their hair into damp spikes. "You like?"

It was dyed. Stripes of bright blue, pale pink, and pure white. It was strangely bright—and Ashraf scowled.

"What'd you do that for?"

"It's pretty!"

"Your hair was pretty," Ashraf said mournfully.

"Aw." Jamie made a cooing noise and stooped to kiss him on their way past the bed to the mirror. Despite the teasing, the kiss was soft and sweet. "Come out with me," they whispered.

Ashraf hesitated. They were buoyant and bubbly. At their best. He wanted to see it.

Except maybe for the hair.

"It washes out, right?"

"Yup."

Ashraf grumbled, tugging on it a little. Jamie laughed. They broke away to wriggle into a pair of tight leather trousers and rummage in another drawer.

"What you looking for?"

"My packer."

"Sock drawer. I washed it last week."

"Ooh, thanks."

The idea seemed to be a gender mindfuck. Ashraf knew that Tabitha had been scared of being stared at and standing out, and had asked everyone to come looking nice and outlandish to take the pressure off her. He should have known Jamie would to rise to the occasion.

The tight leather pants and the packer were unmistakeably masculine. The six-inch heels on the thigh-high hooker boots hovered in the middle, thanks to Jamie's oddly large feet. But when they produced a roll of modesty tape from the sock drawer and began to carefully cut out hearts to stick over their nipples, he knew exactly where they were going. Only one club in town that allowed topless dancing.

And all right, it was a good decision for a gender reveal party—being queer as hell, and the clientele more interested in grass and speed than gender and sexuality—but it was off the main thoroughfare. There was a long, dark walk back to the taxi ranks from the club doors.

Ashraf sighed.

"All right," he said. "I'll come."

Jamie—preening in the mirror in their leather pants, trans flag hair, and two pieces of tape—*beamed*.

IT WAS HALF past one before Ashraf drained his last Coke and decided he'd had enough. There were only so many times he could take being flirted with by drunken strangers at a urinal.

He abandoned his post at the bar and waded into the sea of bodies on the dance floor, Jamie's abandoned jacket over his arm. They were gyrating in their trousers and thigh-highs, half the eyes of the room on them and their so-called modesty tape, and the sweat gleamed on every inch of skin. The trans flag was dark and damp in the flashing light, and Ashraf smiled. Nobody had a clue what Jamie's birth certificate said, and they'd be smug as hell to know it.

Still, he'd have to tell them in the morning. They'd been knocking back enough shots they'd never remember if he told them now.

He went for bold and grabbed their body in a bear hug, kissing their neck before shouting, "C'mon, beautiful! My turn!"

Jamie wriggled. When he let go, they turned and looped their arms around his neck, a clumsy kiss landing on his mouth.

"You going to take me home?"

"That's the idea."

They grinned. Their eyes were bleary, and they swayed on their feet as Ashraf steered them towards the door. The party had gone well. Everyone was smashed, happy, and pairing off. Jamie whined, but let Ashraf zip them into their jacket in exchange for a few messy kisses at the club door and a soft stroke over one breast that said loud and clear their first stop when they got home would be the bathroom, and not for the usual reasons.

"C'mon, drinky," he said, as the cold night air made them reel and cling to his arm. "Just up the lane and we'll flag down a cab."

"Dance wi' me..."

He found himself tugged into a strange slow dance in the middle of the lonely road, and laughed, kissing the top of their head.

"Nope, c'mon, not in the road."

"Ash? Love you."

"I know," he said, squeezing an arm around their shoulders and nuzzling their obscenely coloured hair. "I love you too."

"Tabby was dead pleased to see you."

"Good."

"She said you're a keeper."

"Am I?"

"Yup."

Fingers toyed with the buttons on his coat, and he nudged them away gently.

"I want to keep you," they said and stretched up to kiss his cheek. "For good."

Ashraf smiled. "Me too, sweetheart."

"M'sorry it's hard."

"Eh?"

"Being with me."

"Oh hey, it's not," he said as they reached the top of the lane, and he hooked his fingers into Jamie's belt loops to make sure they wouldn't stagger in front of any cars. "It's not hard."

"We don't fit but we do fit and it's hard."

"That makes no sense," he said easily and gave them a one-sided hug while waiting for the lights to change and let them cross. "Getting past the hydrophobia is hard. Putting up with your mate Shane is hard. But then I get every Sunday morning cuddled up in bed with you, and get to see you raving and ranting at the TV most evenings, and it's so easy."

Even as he said it, he found his thoughts rearranging themselves in his head. It *was* easy, being with Jamie. They fit even when they shouldn't, and it had been that way from the very beginning. They never batted an eyelash at the lack of alcohol in his life, at the prayer mat and Qur'an in the living room, at the sex-free zone that his bedroom had been for his entire life. They smiled when he cracked bad jokes, and laughed at the telly with him, and cuddled up to him like he was the centre of their universe. Even though he didn't care about fish, didn't like the water, and wasn't remotely interested in queer politics.

Maybe it wasn't Jamie he needed to defeat the hydrophobia for after all.

Chapter Twenty

"OKAY," JAMIE SAID, sliding in beside him. Their goggles were around their neck, and their cap in place. Ready to swim—but ready to get out again, too. "You ready to try this?"

Ashraf tightened his grip on the side and looked down the pool. It was the first Wednesday of April. They'd been trying this for months now, and he'd only progressed to standing in the pool—not moving, clinging to the side—in all that time.

And he'd had enough.

"Same depth all the way?"

"Yup."

"And I can just get out midway?"

"Yep."

"And—"

"Ashraf. You can hold on to the side the whole way. You can get out whenever. This is just—awkward walking."

"Awkward?"

Jamie smiled. "You've clearly forgotten how hard walking in water is. C'mon!"

Ashraf decided to be absolutely shameless. He wasn't ready to do it. It was just Jamie being all bright and breezy that was getting him this far. So they could put up and shut up—he reached out and slid his fingers through theirs.

"Walk with me."

They raised their eyebrows, but squeezed his hand and stopped treading water, rising slightly as their feet hit the bottom and they straightened up.

"Okay. *If* you start soon. We're not all superheated on testosterone, you know. This water's chilly."

"Shouldn't that be me who's cold, then, if I'm running hotter?"

"Oh yeah. Then move. Can't let you get cold, you'll get out."

Ashraf managed a shaky laugh—and let go of the side.

It felt silly to be startled that nothing happened, because of course it didn't. He was standing in water that only reached his chest. It didn't even cover his surgery scars. What could possibly happen?

The bolt of relief was intense anyway, and when Jamie tugged lightly, he had to take a deep breath before pushing his foot forward through the water and taking that first step.

And it was—fine.

Surprisingly fine. The pool was quiet, a couple of elderly ladies doing breaststroke in another lane and nobody else around. The water lapped at his skin hopefully, but didn't tug him down or back. It flowed passively around him, uncaring, and the second breath didn't feel so ragged.

"That's it," Jamie said gently. "See? Nice and easy."

It was. It was terrifying, too—his heart was beating a mile a minute, and he thought he was going to be sick—but it was also easy. It *was* just like walking awkwardly. And in a way, it was...nice, too. He'd not only forgotten how hard walking in water was, but also the pleasure in doing so. He'd forgotten how nice the buoyancy felt. He'd forgotten how light he could feel in water without getting spikes of dysphoria.

"C'mon," Jamie said. "You're halfway."

He looked up. They were right. Halfway already. The pool had seemed so long, sitting on the side and watching Jamie swim. But it wasn't really. He was keeping pace with an old man doing a determined doggy paddle in the next lane. He might have his feet on the floor, but he was moving through water just as much as the man was.

Only he must look a sight. One hand was still hovering near the side, ready to grab. The other was gripping Jamie's like a vice. And he was walking like he'd only just learned.

"You'd think I didn't know how to swim," he groused.

"Any time you want to try that, I'm good," Jamie said easily. "Ten more steps!"

One, two, three—

"You have the patience of a saint," Ashraf said.

"Ooh, talk flirty to me, baby," Jamie teased. "Also I looked in my swimming book last night."

"Yeah?"

"You've been doodling."

"I've been *writing*, thank you very much," Ashraf said— and seized the end of the pool.

"Uh-uh," Jamie said, tugging his fingers free again and turning him around. "C'mon. Back we go."

"Seriously?"

"Yes!" They pulled. "And what were you writing?"

Ashraf swallowed and stepped forward. Jamie had both his hands. He couldn't reach for the side. He could feel his breathing getting tighter.

"I—uh—"

"It looks like drawings."

"It's not," he croaked. "It's Arabic. Well, b-badly written Arabic, anyway, my handwriting is crap..."

"What does it say?"

"Depends on the page."

"Tell me all of it."

"I don't remember all of it," he said. "The—the first day, I remember that one. That one was easy. It was a line from that poem you liked."

"Ooh, I like," Jamie said. "If you write it all beautifully for me, I'm going to get it tattooed on me."

Ashraf wrinkled his nose. "I don't like tattoos."

"Tough. I love them. They're gorgeous."

"You can't improve perfection."

"Very cheesy," Jamie said. "Hey, write me *that* in Arabic and I'll get it as a tattoo as well."

"Urgh."

"You're the one always saying Arabic is a beautiful language."

"A beautiful *spoken* language."

"I beg to differ. You said the mosque is beautiful, and that's only got words in it, right? And I think you could make great art with Arabic writing; it looks stunning."

"Because you can't read it. You think it looks exotic."

"Well, yeah, but you can make great art with the Roman alphabet too."

"For a biologist, I'm impressed you know English uses the Roman alphabet."

"I'm a scientist, not completely culturally stupid," Jamie said loftily. "Anyway, *I'm* not the one who can be distracted by a bit of chatting-up about Arabic."

"What?"

"We're on your third lap."

Ashraf stopped dead in the middle of the pool and blinked at the clock ahead of them on the wall. They'd turned round again. They were headed back towards the windows, away from the changing rooms.

Third length.

"You sneaky little—"

Jamie grinned and nosed in for a quick kiss. "Four lengths," they whispered against his mouth, "and when we go home, I will give you a marker pen and you can write all the Arabic, all over me, whatever and wherever you want."

Ashraf swallowed and started to walk again.

"What—what do I get if I manage six lengths?"

"Same deal."

"Eight lengths?"

"I promise not to get any of it tattooed on me."

Ashraf blew out his cheeks and nodded.

"Right," he said. "Ten lengths it is. And then I'm going to go and faint in the sauna for an *hour*."

HE ONLY MANAGED six lengths, but Jamie made the tattoo promise anyway, before stripping naked and lying on their front on the rug in the living room, head propped up on their folded arms to watch *Stargate*, and leaving Ashraf with a marker pen and five foot three inches of opportunities.

And he didn't know what to write.

Most of the Arabic in the swimming book *was* little more than doodles, aside from that initial line of poetry. He'd written all the feelings Jamie gave him—love, happiness, peace—and all the things Jamie was—sneaky, difficult, beautiful, amazing—and, on a particularly bad day, a long series of complex words dredged out of the back of his mind that he could barely spell, so he'd have to focus hard on the letters forming under his pen rather than the water lapping at his legs.

But kneeling on the carpet by Jamie's prone form, nothing came to mind.

"Stuck?" Jamie asked absently as the credits rolled and the adverts starting playing.

"Mm."

They tipped a bare foot up. "Start there. Anything that'll fit."

Ashraf blinked, then took the foot in one hand.

"All right. Stay still."

"Wha—*Oh my God, that is not where I meant!*"

The indignant yowl was worth every second of the struggle to write the Arabic word for foot on the sole of the aforementioned appendage. Jamie was wildly ticklish, and squirmed magnificently under him, forcing Ashraf to clamp their leg between his thighs to hold it still.

"Don't make me bite your toes," he warned as he finished, and was sworn at. "Right. Give me the other one."

"Noooo!"

He wrote 'bad' on the bottom of that foot, then turned them both over, held them down on the floor between his knees, and wrote 'disobedient' across both of them.

That inspired him, and he turned Jamie back over to write 'sin' and 'forbidden' on one arse-cheek each, before flipping them onto their back and writing 'beautiful' and 'perfect' on each face-cheek. Jamie started to laugh and demand kisses, and it all dissolved into a strange game that was both oddly sexual and oddly chaste at the same time, as Jamie peppered him with kisses and Ashraf wrote everything from 'this is impossible' to 'a gift from God' on their body in various places. He named the tiny, almost invisible scar from their breast reduction, called their bikini line the forbidden place, and decorated their left thigh in several lines from their favourite English poem. It turned out to be fiendishly difficult to translate Burns into Arabic, but it was worth the shoddy job by the way Jamie quieted and watched him work, a soft and affectionate expression evident in their eyes.

So when he capped the pen, he crawled over them and dipped in for a kiss, for once dropping his hips to rest between their legs.

"You're a mess," he said.

"But you love me."

"I love you *because* you're a mess," he corrected, and they laughed.

"You *sure* I can't get any of these tattooed into place?"

"Yes. You're too beautiful for ink."

"Ink *is* beautiful," they whined but nuzzled their nose against his cheek. "Pick one or I will."

"You're really going to do it, aren't you?"

"Yes."

He hesitated, shifting back to touch them all in turn, finding the best one, the most appropriate one, before finally settling on the one he'd painstakingly shaded into being on the space of rib under their left arm, just shy of the swell of their breast.

"This one," he said, stroking it lightly and watching them blink, momentarily distracted.

"Um. What does it say?"

He bent to kiss them again, catching his lips against theirs in a soft graze. They lay passive, and let him tug with his teeth before letting go, and only then did they smile.

"What does it *say*?" they persisted softly, and Ashraf laughed quietly.

"Fish."

Jamie made an outraged cry and struck out, turning the soft moment into another wrestling match that smudged all of his careful work—but it was worth it.

Cuddled up on the rug after, dragging the blankets down off the sofa because they were both too lazy to get up, stroking Jamie's breast gently as they watched their next TV show from his shoulder—it was worth it.

He'd walk a thousand pools for this, whenever Jamie asked.

Chapter Twenty-One

THE KNOCK ON his door came with five minutes left in his office hours, and Ashraf groaned.

"Come in," he grumbled, already mentally cursing whichever student was on the other side.

It cracked open, and blonde hair appeared in the gap.

"Ashraf?"

His hand stiffened on the mouse. Oh, *hell*.

"Kath."

She edged into the gap, glancing around. Unfortunately, being his office hours, the other lecturers had cleared off.

"Are you busy?"

"It's my office hours."

"Yes, I know," she said pointedly. "That's how I knew you'd be here. But you haven't got a student, so..."

She shut the door with a snap behind her and pulled out the chair across from his desk.

"Fine," he snapped, saving his edits to his paper. "What can I help you with?"

"I wanted to talk to you."

"Our research interests don't align. If it's about a student, you're better talking to Callahan; if it's about Jamie, then I'm not interested," he said coolly. "Please leave."

"I want to clear the air."

"I don't. Please leave."

"I think you took my concerns the wrong way."

His jaw clenched. "Leave."

"It wasn't about you."

Ashraf sat back, folding his arms across his chest. So what if he looked belligerent? He felt it well enough.

"Yes, so you said. Repeatedly. That you were just concerned for Jamie."

"I was."

"Were you?" he demanded. "You never tried to talk to Jamie on their own. You constantly misgendered them in my presence, so you can't have been paying them that much attention. You can't have been awake at night worrying about them."

A scowl flashed across her face before she pursed her lips and then carefully smoothed out her features.

"I don't want to rehash all of that," she retorted. "I was concerned there was something going on which might be...harmful for one of our students, and—"

"One of whose students?"

"The university's."

"Really. And how did you know Jamie was a student here?"

"Because—because you mentioned they were doing a PhD."

"Could have been doing it at Durham."

"You said you met them at debate club."

"Could have been at Northumbria."

She swallowed. "I take your point. But they weren't."

He raised his eyebrows.

"You can't blame me for trying to look out for a student."

"No," he admitted. "I can't. What I can blame you for is the assumptions you were making, the prejudices you were using, to think there was something wrong in the first place."

"Like?"

"We've been over this."

"You accused me of being a racist."

"Must be nice," he said tightly. "You're busier being pissed I called you racist than wondering why I could have thought that in the first place."

"It was nothing to do with you being—"

She stopped. Ashraf cocked his head.

"What? Italian? Egyptian? Muslim?"

She snorted. "Any of it."

"Really," he said. It wasn't a question. "So if it had been Tom, you would have had the same objections?"

"Yes."

"*Really*?" he pressed. "Because being perfectly honest here, Kath, I don't believe you. If Jamie had been Muslim as well, would that have been all right?"

"What does—"

"If they'd been she, if they'd been a nice Muslim girl from—well, anywhere, pick a country—would that have been all right? If I'd been seeing a nice twenty-four-year-old girl from Egypt, from where my mother was from, as she would have undoubtedly wanted if she was still alive?"

"That's a cultural issue," she said, and Ashraf shook his head.

"Love's not a cultural issue," he said, "and that your first objection was the age gap and Jamie being a student, but you'd waive it for a Muslim student...that says a lot."

"You're wrong," she replied. "But I didn't want to come here to discuss that. I wanted to clear the air, and—"

"Clear the air?" he asked. "No. I can't clear the air with someone who complains about my romantic relationships if they're with white people."

"Ex*cuse* me?"

"You heard," he snapped. "You'd give me a pass if Jamie were a Muslim girl. Because they're not, it's a problem. Well, that's *your* problem. Nobody else seems to think there's an issue."

"Nobody else thinking there's an issue could be used to defend a lot of things."

"In this case, it rightly means there isn't one," he said. "If you have any further complaints, take them up with Callahan. Please leave my office now."

"Why are you being so—"

"What?" he retorted. "Obstinate? Difficult? Stubborn? Pick one. I don't have to justify my relationship to anyone who thinks it's wrong based on my faith or where I'm from."

"It's not about—"

"Except it is. If you'd bothered to talk to Jamie—or to me, instead of making snide remarks—then you would have known it wasn't what you thought."

And he could prove it. Then and there, he could prove it. Tell her about Jamie helping him with his hydrophobia. Tell her about his sexual orientation, and the complete lack of power he held when it came to sex and sexual relationships. Tell her about his own transition, and how he was just as supposedly vulnerable as Jamie when it came to intimate relationships.

But why?

Why should he have to tell her anything? Why did he have to prove anything? It wouldn't have been an accusation levied at him before he transitioned, because only men were predators. It wouldn't have been something she would have thought if she knew or understood asexuality, because asexual people were the weak ones in relationships. It wouldn't even have been an issue if she knew he was trans, because everybody knew trans men were sexless beings, and effectively just women no matter the size of the beard or the length of the cock.

He'd heard it all before.

"Right," he said, standing up and grabbing his coat off the back of his chair. "Either you leave my office, right now, or I do. Pick one."

"I'm not done—"

"I am!" he thundered. "I am done, Kath! You don't get to just throw your judgement of my relationships in my face when you know jack shit about them—while you're getting off on saving some poor queer student from someone like me—and then come in here pretending you're the victim. Because I've had enough of that shit!"

She swelled up like a bullfrog, and he stormed past her. When he jerked the door open, his new officemate Professor Ryan had her hand inches from the doorknob. She blinked owlishly at him.

"Getting coffee," he ground out and stalked off down the corridor.

"Ashraf!"

Maybe not coffee, then. He scrubbed that idea and changed it. Callahan's office, he decided, as he began to jog up the stairs two at time. He'd been toying with the idea, but if Kath was going to start chasing some kind of absolution for what she'd done, then he was out. He'd find another posting. Even if he had to fall back on tutoring Italian for the languages department again. He didn't need to stick around for this.

Callahan wasn't in his office—of course—but Ashraf let himself in anyway, shutting the door on any witnesses and sitting down in the chair to write a note. A long note. Threatening resignation if Kath harassed him anymore, or if Callahan tried to push him to forgive her. Not a chance.

Once the note was written and taped to his computer monitor where Callahan would have to deal with it, Ashraf sat back and went straight to the favourites list on his phone.

Ashraf: *Rough day. Spa session?*

Jamie: *Ooh which spa? xxx*

Ashraf: *Was thinking the hydrotherapy pool in the leisure centre. Want to help me get in there?*

Jamie: *You sure? The jets are lively, the water does burst in your face sometimes xxx*

Ashraf: *I'm sure. I might even try an actual swim.*

Jamie: *This sounds like a really rough day :(You okay? xxx*

Ashraf: *Will be once I get a kiss off you. Kath came by my office and started spouting bollocks. Need to just not be at work or thinking about it.*

Jamie: *I'll come and slap her at your next big departmental meeting! I'm in labs until two but I was going to go to the leisure centre after anyway so why don't you treat yourself to a good lunch and meet me at the Metro station at two fifteen? xxx*

Ashraf: *Deal. See you soon x*

Jamie: *Yep love you! xxx*

"SO I'M THINKING of just quitting and getting a posting somewhere else," Ashraf finished.

He was standing in the pool, having walked eight lengths while ranting to Jamie, who had swum leisurely along beside him on their back. They weren't wearing their cap, and the halo of hair—brown again at long last—was enticing and pretty, but he didn't quite dare touch it for fear of pushing their head under.

"Don't," they said, turning to brace their feet on the pool wall and beginning to circle their arms in half the act of treading water.

"Why?"

"Because if you do, you're letting a bigot chase you out."

Ashraf opened his mouth...and closed it again.

"If we quit every time a bigot showed their ugly mug, we'd never get anywhere," Jamie said. "You know how shit my undergraduate thesis supervisor was with me. If I'd just quit then..."

"Then you'd not be here."

"Yeah. And—I hate to say it, but you've faced down worse and you will again. We both know you will."

Ashraf grimaced. Yeah. As long as Islamophobia was the fashionable bigotry for the British media, he would face it again. And again and again and again.

"You'd never travel anywhere because of the shit you get in airports, you'd never have transitioned because of all the bigots saying you never should, you'd never have said yes when I kissed you, even, because of all the people who've said you're bust because you're ace."

Ashraf blew out his cheeks.

"And you'd not have finished your first degree, or stayed at university, or kissed me in the first place," he said quietly.

"Yep."

"So you're saying there's always a silver lining?"

"Always something good that *could* come out of it, in the end. I think you're right not to roll over and forgive her," Jamie said, "but don't let her shove you out either. If anyone shouldn't be there, it's her if she's got views like that."

"Mamma used to say people wouldn't learn if you did that every time."

"Yeah, well, your mamma didn't get dragged into an HR meeting with people accusing your boyfriend of grossness," Jamie said tartly. They pushed off lightly and floated like a pale starfish in the water in front of him. "Screw her."

"No thanks."

They laughed, sank, and came back up in a splash. "Not literally! Berk."

"You walked into that one."

"Swam into it."

"Oh, ha bloody ha."

"Ba-dum-tsh," Jamie muttered and began to starfish again. "Stick it out. Put in a counter-complaint that she's harassing you, and say you'll take it higher if she doesn't leave you alone."

Ashraf chuckled. "And when did you get so well-versed in how to play the system to punish a dickhead?"

"*You* try getting a public body to use non-binary pronouns."

"Touché, but I'd settle for them spelling my name right."

"Well, that's your fault," Jamie said smugly. "Everyone can spell Singer. If we ever got married, you should change yours."

Ashraf blinked, mentally drawing a ring around Jamie's third finger, then shook himself and hunched lower in the water.

"Hey."

"What?" Jamie asked lazily.

"I'm going to try swimming."

That got their attention, and they pushed their hips down, righting themself to tread water in front of him.

"Yeah?"

"Yeah."

He felt—brave. Buoyed. Determined to be as blasé as Jamie about this, even if he couldn't be about Kath. If twats still got under his skin, he ought to drive out the hydrophobia to make more room for them. One hatred at a time, right?

"Back up," he said.

Jamie grinned, and kicked out, drifting off up the pool for perhaps five metres before stopping.

"If you swim over here," they called, "then I'll give you a water kiss! Like in all the slushy movies you pretend not to like!"

Ashraf narrowed his eyes. Accusation of slushy movie liking? No chance.

And it was like—riding a bicycle.

The feeling of his feet on the wall tiles.

The stretch of his shoulders in the right position.

The water touching his chin.

He kicked.

Launched.

Floated.

And *swam*.

Chapter Twenty-Two

HE TOOK JAMIE'S advice.

He had an application half-completed for Northumbria, but parked it up and waited to see what Callahan would do.

Practically nothing, as it turned out. He emailed acknowledging the note and saying he'd talk to Kath, but that was all.

But Kath didn't return to his office. He got a text off Tom a couple of days after their argument saying she was in a right mood and did Ashraf have anything to do with it, and that was all.

And that was—almost worse than another argument.

Ashraf was no stranger to bigotry—couldn't be, at the intersection of all the things that made up his existence—but the part he hated the most was where it all came down to him. If he did nothing, it would be his fault if things carried on. If he spoke up, it was his fault for making things awkward or difficult. If he forgave people for their so-called mistakes, it was his fault if they never learned, but if he didn't forgive at all, it was his fault that they supposedly couldn't learn.

He was *tired* of it all.

On the upside, his new office was empty more often than not, and the one time that Professor Ryan walked in to see Jamie sitting on his desk in a very short skirt and talking a mile a minute about a new wetsuit they'd seen online—that they were not subtly asking Ashraf to loan them money to buy—she had merely said hello and asked them to stop banging their heels off the drawers because it was annoying.

"Oh, sure, sorry," Jamie said and flashed Ashraf a little thumbs up.

Professor Ryan—Alison, but she was so stern and severe-looking that it felt odd to call her that—didn't seem to give a damn about anything in the office except smelly food and repetitive noises. The third occupant of the tiny little room, a research assistant called Parveen, seemed to be an invisible ghost. Her things came and went, but the most Ashraf ever saw of her was a skirt disappearing around the side of a rapidly closing door.

It was lonelier than the old office, but at least he didn't have to face a second round of bullshit about his relationship with Jamie from his new cohabitants.

In fact, it took a week before Callahan came back with anything more than the original acknowledgement, and his eventual reply wasn't any more inspiring than his original one.

Ashraf,

I've talked to Kath again, and she's agreed it wouldn't be appropriate of her to approach you right now. Clearly, everything is a bit raw and everyone is a bit het up. I've asked her to not approach you directly, although, obviously, you do work in the same department and there's nothing I can do about campus. We can't start banning each other from various communal areas, after all!

For my part, I don't believe there was anything malicious in what Kath thought—

Ashraf snorted. "Sure," he muttered at the computer. "Because since when did a cis, straight, white guy know what bigotry looked like?"

—but she obviously overstepped the mark, and I can see how it may have looked to you. In the end though, please remember she was trying to look out for a student. I genuinely think she only had good intentions.

"Yeah, well, road to hell."

"Ashraf, if you *must* talk to your computer, could you at least let the rest of us in on the conversation?" Professor Ryan asked, and Ashraf jumped.

"Er. Sorry."

"Problem?"

"Er. Complaint. About—another member of staff. That I have. Er."

"Oh, yes, I heard. Kathleen." Professor Ryan waved a hand. "Never had anything to do with her. Can't imagine Callahan is much use though."

Ashraf blinked. "Er. Well. No."

"He's as useful as a chocolate fireman," she muttered, prodding her keyboard and squinting at her screen like it was sending her rude messages. "Something about your other half, wasn't it?"

"Uh. Yes. Kath thought it was...inappropriate."

"Wasn't that your other half in here the other week?"

"Yes..." Ashraf said warily.

"The skirt was inappropriate, I'll give her that. Frightful colour."

Ashraf barked a laugh. "Uh. No. Not the skirt. Jamie's a PhD student."

That earned him a sharp look.

"Reading?"

"Marine biology."

"Oh." Another dismissive wave. "Irrelevant, then."

Ashraf blinked. "Yeah...yeah, it is."

"Ah!" A crooked finger waved in the air, even as her gaze went back to the computer. "Let me guess. There was a cultural element to the matter."

Ashraf raised his eyebrows. "Seriously?"

"Am I right?"

"Yeah, but..."

"We're not all blind," she said and clicked her tongue at him. "My son-in-law is from Pakistan. Very devout Muslim, apart from the moment where he married my daughter."

"Oh. *Oh.*"

"My husband was very much the same. Deeply inappropriate, this Muslim lad chasing after our Dawn."

Privately, Ashraf thought she was lucky anyone had chased after anybody unfortunate enough to be named Dawn.

"Same nonsense. Your Jamie looks good for you."

"Eh?"

"You're too serious," she said and flashed him a smirk over her monitor. "Now, you're young. Get over here and make this damned machine print this email."

Ashraf rolled his eyes—both at being called too serious and being called young—but heaved himself to his feet.

"You've probably printed a thousand copies in the Dean's office or something," he groused as he made his way over, but smiled on the inside.

Maybe Jamie was right. Maybe there *was* always a positive outcome, somewhere along the way.

ASHRAF WENT TO Fajr at the mosque the next morning.

He almost never did. Morning prayer was a private affair, to him. Even Mamma, devout as she'd been, hadn't gone to mosque for Fajr. But that morning, he left a note for Jamie and crept out before dawn, cycling in lieu of a bus. The imam had looked pleased, but startled, and didn't seem to quite believe him when he said everything was fine.

"I just need a bit of courage today," Ashraf said. "I'm going to try doing something I'm afraid of."

"Something good, I hope?"

"Yes."

The quietness of the mosque in early morning seemed to amplify its warmth and welcome. Ashraf felt sombre as he prayed, but buoyed as he left. Allah approved, he was certain. Allah would be watching out for him.

He cycled out to the leisure centre rather than getting the first of the Metro trains heading out that way. The bracing breeze helped clear the sleepiness and added a steely edge to the resolve the mosque had given him. He was going to achieve something today, however small. He had his lofty goal, but if all he achieved was the first step, then it was still an important step. It was still vital.

The leisure centre opened at six for the early-morning gym bunnies, and Ashraf found himself changing in a room full of elderly men with insomnia and steroid abusers who had to crush themselves into suits and office chairs by nine. And probably, by the grumpy expressions and cheap protein shakes, at call centres and customer service desks all across the city.

Ashraf stripped, stepped into his trunks, and took a deep breath before closing his locker.

"You can do this," he told the padlock. "You've done it before."

But with Jamie.

Which was rather the point of this morning.

The pool was empty when he walked out onto the tiles. Still. Perfect. The filters humming loudly, and the water not quite completely warmed yet. He put his towel in the usual place. Sat on the side, cross-legged, while he forced his frizz into the cap. Slid his shins into the water when he moved on to his goggles.

And stopped.

Just stopped, sitting on the side on his own. Alone. No Jamie to smile and encourage him. No Jamie to distract him from the enormity of where he was.

On the side of an enormous bowl of water, with his heart in his throat.

"You can do this," Ashraf told himself—and pushed off.

He slid into the pool with barely a ripple. The cold water was a shock. It surged up his skin, smoothing out his beard, destroying his weight. When he held onto the side, his legs rose of their own accord. He half floated, holding his breath like he might crash to the bottom any minute.

And grinned.

The euphoria was sharp and intense. He'd gotten into the pool. Not six months ago, he couldn't even step onto the beach in Jordan without wanting to throw up, and that had been with Jamie's hand in his own. And now here he was. Floating in the corner of a swimming pool, on his own.

But that hadn't been the point.

"Okay," he said and turned his legs the other way. Pressed them up against the pool wall, and jutted his chin out against the surface of the water. "You can do this. You can swim fine. You know that."

A woman walking past to use another lane gave him a funny look, but he ignored her. So what if he looked crazy?

He was going to do this. And when he'd done this, he'd know that he could overcome this fear enough to mesh with Jamie's life properly. If he could swim on his own, then he could close the gap between them. Maybe he'd never beat the sea—but he'd beat the water.

Ashraf blew out his cheeks, sucked in a breath—and kicked.

The first dizzying launch from the side was terrifying. His lungs exploded. His heart burst. His shoulder surged down in the water—then rose, like a boat hitting a wave. His arms flew forward. His heels tucked up to his crotch and kicked out, and—

He swam.

He *swam*.

It was clumsy. He crashed through the water. He kept his eyes fixed on the opposite wall. The clock ticking above it. They bobbed up and down as he struck out. As his palms came back into his chest, only to bounce back out. As his knees arched sideways and the frog-like kick began to get smoother. Simpler. Less exhausting.

Less terrifying.

Because the wall was getting closer. He could make out the individual numbers on the clock. His breathing began to match the rhythm of the stroke, forced into line by the way his shoulders and ribs moved. He could feel his stomach sag, and the instinctive hitching upwards of his arse to counteract it.

He was swimming.

On his own.

He was *swimming*.

He lashed out, fingers slipping on the edge of the pool, and it was done. He'd swum a whole length, completely on his own. His heart was thundering in his ears, and he was gulping for air that was nothing to do with the exercise. He'd done harder cycling routes to work during the roadworks last summer.

But cycling didn't come with this kind of high.

Ashraf rested his forehead on the edge and laughed giddily at the shaking water under his face. "You lose," he told it and laughed again. He could swim again. He could *swim.*

And when he turned to stare back up the pool, at the churning wake he'd left behind, he couldn't even find it within himself to feel embarrassed or stupid about it. It was the farthest he'd swum since he was nine. And all right, it wasn't the sea, but it was still a pool. It was a freshwater pool at that, with none of the buoyancy aid of salt water. After all these years, he had gotten into the water, on his own, and swum an entire length.

What would Jamie say?

He tightened his grip on the side.

Jamie swam between fifty and seventy-five lengths every time they came to the pool. They were shockingly fit. If Ashraf were sexual, he'd not be able to watch that beautiful body cutting through the water, right where it belonged. And he'd never be up to seventy-five lengths on the trot—wasn't fit enough, had no ambition to be fit enough—but perhaps next time they went on holiday, he could keep up a little in the pool. Perhaps they could mess around like Jamie had wanted to in Jordan. Perhaps they could be like those couples on romantic hotel adverts, who cuddled while swimming around, kissing without a care for where they actually were.

Water cuddles. Floating weightless, with nothing but Jamie to hold onto.

The idea was more than enticing—it was addictive. A whole new goal.

"Ten laps," he told himself and twisted around to get back into position. "One down, nine to go."

He kicked, soared back into the water, and began to splash for the other end.

One down, nine to go.

Chapter Twenty-Three

THE POOL WAS one thing—but it wasn't the sea.

It didn't smell of salt and seaweed. It didn't swell and surge. It just lay there, a flat expanse in a rectangular confinement. Artificial. False. *Calm.*

Swimming a length of a pool didn't mean he could do anything about the sea. And swimming pools had never been the problem. Jamie didn't go on holidays so they could dive in a swimming pool. They went for coral reefs and crashing waves. The *sea.*

He had to tackle the sea.

The opportunity didn't arise for a while. The spring was well and truly underway, and it was the worst time to be a lecturer. The students started panicking and actually used office hours as exam season approached, and—to top it off— Callahan was trying to get on his good side again. He'd obviously heard about Ashraf making enquiries at Durham. Unfortunately, it meant that Ashraf was being invited to a lot of meetings, a blatant hint of potential promotion, and he wanted no part of it.

So it was May before the beach beckoned. Specifically, the fourteenth. Even more specifically, a full three hundred and sixty-five days since Jamie had asked Ashraf to walk them to the bus stop after debate club and kissed him under the electronic timetable.

One full year.

A year ago, Ashraf had found himself staring slack-jawed at a blushing MSc student he was on little more than nodding terms with, and mentally reaching for his polite, "Sorry but I'm just not interested." Only, for the first time, it hadn't been entirely true. A year ago, he'd been derailed. His staunch aromanticism had given way to a cloudier space in the grey-romantic world, and he'd spent the entire time Jamie was in Australia wondering why he was missing them. A year ago, he'd turned out to not quite be who he'd thought he was. And a year later, he didn't mind a moment of it.

The fourteenth was a Tuesday, and Ashraf left the office early with a vague plan in mind. Neither of them really did celebrations—Jamie had mentioned getting their favourite takeaway and a cuddle in front of Ashraf's favourite film as their big plan for the evening—but Ashraf decided to dare. Jamie was right, that morning in Aqaba. Ashraf did think of this as permanent.

And if he wanted to have anniversary takeaways for all the other Mays throughout the rest of his life, he needed to make some progress beyond a calm swimming pool and a white noise machine.

So he headed over to the biology building with a plan in mind.

He found Jamie in their usual lab, bent over a tank with George and discussing...something scientific. Ashraf rapped his knuckles on the metal as he pushed open the door, and earned himself a startled look.

"What's—oh my God, it can't be five already!"

"Half four, actually," Ashraf said. "Can the fish wait one day?"

Jamie pulled a face as they shrugged off their lab coat. "I'm so sorry; I meant to come and meet you after my two o'clock, but George got a call from the Australian team and—"

"It's fine," Ashraf said. "Not like we have reservations anywhere. I just have an idea that might be nice. C'mon."

Jamie bounced around the lab stashing their toys away, chattering nineteen to the dozen at George, who didn't look up once from his overflowing binder of notes and intense perusal of the tank. Ashraf pulled himself up on a stool to wait peaceably, absorbing the rhythm of Jamie's words yet none of their meaning. It was just like that white noise machine.

When they were done, bag thrown over their shoulder and pockets patted down for various bits and bats, they launched Ashraf's way, and he caught them—and their kiss—with a smile and a squeeze.

"Hell-*o*!" Jamie enthused, rubbing their cheek against his beard. "Right. All yours!"

"Lucky me," Ashraf deadpanned. "Fancy coming on a little bit of an adventure with me?"

"Sure!"

They were in an effusive mood, and it was catching. The gnawing anxiety in his gut as they boarded the bus out to Whitley Bay didn't get much room around the warm contentment at Jamie's energy. They were dressed fairly masculine—usually were, on lab days—but the constant stream in their high, soft tones made Ashraf brave enough to put an arm around their shoulders, even on a public bus. And their bright happiness even let him smirk at the thought of looking straight enough to get away with it, rather than angry he had to fake it at all.

And they stopped.

"Ash—"

The bus turned the corner onto the coast road, and Ashraf's stomach rolled as a high wave crashed down onto the sand in a wall of white foam.

Jamie's hand found his and squeezed tight.

"Fish and chips on the front," they said, "or a proper sit-down?"

Ashraf swallowed as he pressed the bell. "Whatever you want," he managed in a tight voice, and was quietly grateful when Jamie's hand stayed resolutely in his own until they were both in the confines of the bus shelter, and the bus pulled away with a roar.

Leaving Ashraf staring at the sea.

Despite being an island, the UK was a great place to avoid the sea. It didn't have good enough weather for most of the year, and the beaches weren't much better even if it was warm and sunny. The sea was constantly freezing, usually stormy, and the coastguard were to be found fishing drunk Geordies out of it far more often than holidaymakers. Ashraf had no trouble whatsoever avoiding it entirely.

But there he was. Staring at the sea.

It was windy, the smell of sand and salt in the air. The waves were tall and violent, smashing themselves on the shore like they were at war. All that stood between him and the water was the road and a thin stretch of sand.

Blindly, he tightened his grip on Jamie's hand.

And—breathed.

His heart was hammering, and his stomach felt like he'd been sucker-punched, but he could also breathe. Jamie's thumb was rubbing the side of his knuckles gently. The smell in the air was almost pleasant. And the sound was just like the machine in their bedroom. Rhythmic. Predictable.

Almost strangely soothing, even as it terrified him.

"Okay?" Jamie murmured.

"Think so," Ashraf mumbled.

"You want to look at it from inside a nice, warm restaurant, or you want to get some chippie food and sit on a bench and stare at it like a couple of old ladies?"

Ashraf managed a strangled laugh. "I *want* to try the old ladies on a bench part. Just—might not be able to cross the road to do it."

"Tell you what, then," Jamie said. "Let's get dinner in a proper sit-down place where you can watch the sea and ignore me trying to play footsie with you, and then when we're done, we can walk along the front to that cafe down there and get some ice cream right down by the sand. Double up on dessert."

"Okay. Yeah. That works."

He let Jamie lead the way. Their bright babbling resumed—something about one of Shane's stupid mates trying to go surfing last Christmas off the bay and needing to be rescued by a very irate coastguard crew within ten minutes—and Ashraf let that noise, the warm press of their fingers, and the rumble of the sea carry him through the doors of an Indian restaurant, with great glass windows that beamed out at the sand.

There, he relaxed a little. The constant motion of the sea outside was actually pleasant to watch, where he couldn't smell or hear it. The restaurant was warm and busy, and he could taunt Jamie about their intolerance for spicy food. Their foot ended up tucked between his under the table, and when the evening drew in, they went from brash beauty to soft sweetness, leaning in over the table, their smile dimming to something gentler, and their fingers toying with his between courses.

"I didn't think you'd let me stay a whole year," they said in an almost wistful voice. "I'd nearly talked myself out of asking."

"What changed your mind?"

They shrugged. "Nothing really. Just you kept being really attractive and I kept wanting to kiss you like crazy.

And then when I did, it was the most amazing first kiss I've ever had, so I figured if I didn't ask, I'd regret it forever."

"I know I would."

It had thrown him for a loop. Hell, Jamie just kept throwing him for more loops. He was by the sea having dinner and not a meltdown. He was cohabiting. Next Ramadan, he'd have to stick a standing apology for being a grumpy shit on the fridge.

"I want an honest answer," Jamie said. "I don't care if it's not what I want to hear, I just want you to be really honest with me."

"Okay..."

Jamie bit their lip. "Is this forever for you? I think maybe you think of it as long-term, but...is it for good?"

Ashraf raised his eyebrows.

"I know at first you were really—I don't know, you held back a lot, because you were trying to figure out how you felt and if you were aro or not, and we were both expecting it all to fall apart for a while, so..."

Jamie trailed off, waving a hand absently in the air as they did so. Ashraf reached out to catch it and squeezed both sets of those long, clever fingers on the tablecloth.

Jamie wasn't wrong. The first few months—especially when Jamie had swanned off to Australia—had been a waiting game. Waiting for that strange happiness at Jamie's presence to fade away. Waiting for Jamie to tire of his asexuality. Waiting for whatever odd warmth had erupted between them to cool again.

Only when Jamie had gone, they'd not taken Ashraf's feelings away with them. Instead, he'd found whole new ones. He'd missed them, like he'd never missed anyone in his life before. He'd struggled to sleep on his own. He'd found the house lonely, even though they hadn't lived there then. He'd almost stopped using his phone because Jamie wouldn't be texting him their smileys and exclamation mark addiction all the time.

Then Jamie had come back, as bright and bubbly had ever, and Ashraf had known the feeling in his chest at Heathrow had been love.

He was in love. And staying that way.

"Yes."

"Yes what?"

He squeezed their hands. "Yes, this is a permanent thing for me. Forever. I know what I feel."

Jamie's smile was wobbly at the edges.

"I love you," Ashraf said. "You make me a better person. You dust off the cobwebs when I get too involved in my studies, you remind me to come out of my books now and then, you make me want to face my fears and conquer things. I never went looking for you, or for this, but now you're here, I wouldn't change it for the world."

Jamie leaned over.

"Stop it," they whispered, "or I'm going to cry."

"Mm, fine, but I reserve the right to repeat myself later."

They rolled their eyes as the dessert arrived, and Ashraf smirked at their pinked complexion. When the waitress had retreated again, he tapped his spoon on the table and asked why Jamie wanted to know.

"I just—I don't know. It just feels really permanent, especially since Christmas, and I wanted to know if we were on the same page."

Ashraf nodded, an idea unfolding in the back of his mind. He'd never given much thought to the future when it came to relationships. He'd always assumed there wouldn't be one, and after Jamie had come into his life, he'd spent too much time enjoying it to consider the future in much depth.

What now? He had his career ambitions, his financial goals, his not-so-secret retirement plans when he was old and grey and looking unacceptably similar to his father. But those plans had always been alone, not with Jamie tucked under his shoulder, grinning their irreverently bright smile.

He kept it to himself, though, while they finished dessert and paid their bill, Jamie paying in exchange for a world-class backrub when they got home. They walked out to face the settling dusk and the churning sea, and Ashraf felt a heavy weight over his heart, like a defiant fist was shielding it from the water.

It was just water.

"C'mon," he said. "Let's get an ice cream."

"I think I'm full," Jamie complained. "That cake was insane."

"I could do with one, though. I'll get an extra scoop and we'll split it."

Jamie agreed, tucking their arm into Ashraf's, and they walked along the road together, buffeted by the wind. He barely paused when they crossed to reach the warm lights of the seafront cafe, still barely open against the encroaching night, and he stopped there, on the slope that led down to the sand, staring out at the shimmering blackness of the water.

"Ash?"

He couldn't go down on the beach. He knew that already. Jamie could only bring him so far in one go, and the sand itself was too far. But he was here. Looking at it. Defiant and—mostly—unafraid. He could stand on the front, where he couldn't even glimpse the blue in Jordan without panicking.

"I know it's only been a year—"

"Good year, though."

"—but I really think this is forever, you and me."

Jamie rocked into his side. Ashraf turned on them, cupping their neck in both hands and kissing them, until they were balancing perfectly on their toes to reach.

"I never planned on you, but you happened anyway. And I never planned on asking, but I'm asking anyway."

"Asking wha—"

"If you'll marry me."

Jamie squeaked. Their hands flew up to cover their mouth, and they rocked out of Ashraf's grasp—only to jump right back into it with a shriek, throwing both arms around his neck and clinging until they both crashed into the wall that ran along the front, separating sand from city.

"Oh my God, are you *serious*?"

Ashraf laughed breathlessly, hearing the answer in their glee.

"Yeah," he said and caught both arms around their waist to twirl them around. "I love you and you're amazing and I want to keep you."

They squealed in his ear—then wrenched themself free with a serious expression above a mouth fighting to smile.

"Conditions," they said. "Long engagement."

"Fine."

"And I'm not your wife."

"'Course not."

"And I want to keep my last name."

"Only if I'm allowed to have it too."

Their mouth won the war and exploded into a huge beam. A high noise escaped, and they flung themself on him all over again. Ashraf laughed, his heart thundering in his ears along with the sea.

"Is that a yes?" he asked.

"I changed my mind," Jamie mumbled in his ear. "I want ice cream too."

Chapter Twenty-Four

DAD.

Ashraf paused.

Dear Dad.

No, that was ridiculous.

Hi, Dad.

Better. But now what? Small talk? Launch right in? Somewhere in the middle? Ashraf hadn't done more than exchange birthday cards with his father for years. He talked to his stepmother more oft—

Ah.

He deleted the email entirely and went for the phone. He didn't even have his father's number anymore, but Chiara was resolute about blood family being the most important and had more or less forced them to stay in touch via her.

"Mrs Zaccaria."

Her soft voice, the unusual rhythm of her Venetian accent—even the simple act of hearing Italian instead of English made Ashraf's stomach clench. He loved his country. He missed Italy—the food, the language, the heat, the history—but he didn't miss home. He didn't miss being the one who was wrong, the one who survived, the one who ought to be someone else, the one who ought to be dead. He didn't miss the pressure to be miserable instead of being himself, and he didn't miss the accusing stares his father would give him across the room, like it was the final insult of a displeased God that Ashraf had survived when his perfect sisters had drowned.

He didn't miss any of that.

And yet, slipping into his mother tongue was as comfortable as a good cardigan.

"Hi, Chiara. It's Ashraf."

"Ashraf!" Her voice brightened. "How are you? It's been too long—when are you next visiting? How have you been?"

"Good. I have some news, actually," he said, sitting back in his chair. "I've been seeing someone."

"*Oh!*" He heard her bang a plate down. She was cooking, as always. "Who? What's she like? What's her name? Is she English? Did you—"

"Jamie. And they're not a she."

Only—

Ashraf didn't know any Italian neopronouns. He'd left Italy when he was barely out himself, and far too upset and raw to mix with other trans people. He'd never met an Italian speaker who used neutral or neopronouns, and the sentence that he came out with simply didn't work. He couldn't say what he did and make sense, and the pause on the other end of the line said quite clearly that he'd butchered it.

"Jamie doesn't identify as a man or a woman," he attempted. "They're just a person."

But even then, he couldn't say it right. There wasn't a singular they that he knew of.

"But she must be a man or a woman," Chiara said eventually.

Ashraf gritted his teeth. "That's their *sex*," he said. "They don't identify with that. They haven't got a gender."

There was a long, long pause.

"I don't understand," Chiara said eventually. "Jamie is—Jamie is—"

"Jamie's like me."

"Oh!"

"But not."

"Sorry?"

"Jamie was—" He hated the phrase, but it was probably the only one Chiara would understand. "—born like me. And now they have no gender. Like I'm a man."

It felt wrong to express it that way—any of it—but he'd left Italy before he'd come across non-binary people, and Italian gendered everything. He'd struggled with a singular they in English far more than he'd struggled with neopronouns like xie. And now, not only was he unsure of how to translate it, but Chiara likely wouldn't get it even if she spoke fluent English as well. She could barely wrap her head around Ashraf at the best of times.

"That wasn't my news anyway," he said. "I called to tell you it was our one-year anniversary yesterday."

"Oh, that's nice," she enthused, sounding grateful for the safer territory. "Did you do anything fun?"

"Yes, we got engaged."

She gasped. Then her voice echoed as she pulled the phone away from her ear and shouted, "Nico! Nico! Ashraf is getting married!"

A little chill prickled up his spine at the distant sound of his father's low grumble.

"Not for ages," he said hastily. "Jamie's studying for a PhD and wants to finish that first. It'll be a couple of years yet."

"Still!" she gushed. "It's about time. I always said you were going to end up lonely if you didn't meet someone. Jamie—that's very English, isn't it? Is she Protestant, then?"

Ashraf raised his eyebrows. "No," he said pointedly. "Look, I've got to go. We've got to ring their family too."

"You'll have to come and see us!" Chiara insisted. "Next summer. After Eve."

"Eid."

"Yes, that."

He rolled his eyes. "We'll sort something, Chiara." It stuck in his throat slightly. "Give Dad our love."

"Of course. Love you, Ashraf!"

It rang hollow as he hung up, like it always did, but he pushed it to the back of his mind.

"Jamie!" he called up the stairs. "I told my stepmother. Do you want to ring your mum now?"

"What?"

"Do you want to ring your mum?" he bellowed.

"In English!"

Ashraf opened his mouth—to tell Jamie to open their ears—then realised they were right. Pulling a face, he hauled himself off the sofa and traipsed upstairs to find Jamie the wrong way up on their freshly made bed, feet on the pillows and texting frantically.

"Going to ring your mum?" Ashraf asked, careful to stick to English.

"No need, she already rang me," Jamie said. "I updated my Facebook and it exploded. Beginning to think we should have kept it quiet."

"Who's we?"

They threw him a dirty look.

"It'll have all calmed down by the time we actually plan anything," Ashraf said peaceably. He stretched out beside Jamie, nudging his feet against their own on the pillows. "You want to leave absolutely everything until after you graduate, even the planning?"

"Yeah. Except rings. I want rings. You have to wear one too."

Ashraf shrugged. "I can live with that. Your mum mad?"

"Pretty pissed I told Facebook before her, yep."

"Understandable."

"Whose side are you on?" Jamie whined dramatically, before tossing the phone aside and rolling over until they were lying on top of Ashraf. "One day, I'll make you a Facebook and you'll understand."

"No thanks."

Jamie butted their head against Ashraf's chest, and he smiled, reaching up to card his fingers through their hair. It was getting fairer as summer approached.

"I have a lecture later," he said quietly, "and prayers this evening. Don't want to go all of a sudden."

Jamie grinned. "Go, then when you get back from the mosque tonight, we can celebrate!"

"You mean you want to go out and celebrate with Tabby and Shane."

"Well, yeah."

"Mm, not really up for a Tabby-style celebration," Ashraf said. "How about *you* go celebrate, and I pick you up on my way back from prayers?"

"That'll do," Jamie said and wriggled forward to touch their lips to Ashraf's chin. "When do you have to go?"

"Couple of hours."

"Good. Let's start celebrating now."

ASHRAF GAVE HIS lecture through the happy haze of a food coma.

They'd made proper Scottish tablet, which he'd never had before and now couldn't imagine living without. He'd immediately added a clause to their engagement that a ready supply of tablet had to be arranged, and Jamie had sent him off to deliver his lecture with a laugh.

"You'll get sick of it one day, promise!"

Fat chance. It sat like a heavy, sweet brick in his gut, the contentment overlaying his happiness until even the sight of Tom shuffling into the back of the theatre as the students were dismissed couldn't dim his spirits.

"You're in a good mood," Tom said.

"Yep."

"I saw it on Facebook, actually. Congratulations."

Ashraf's mood lifted a little higher. "Thanks."

"Celebratory brew? On me."

"Yeah, all right."

Things were normal—almost comfortable—as they headed over to the campus cafe, Tom asking how to merge an Italian Muslim wedding with a Scottish Presbyterian one, and Ashraf laughing at him and saying there'd be no houses of worship at all for risk of Jamie catching fire on the threshold.

Then Tom said, "You told Kath you were LGBT."

"I did..."

"And you told me you weren't into men or women."

"Mm."

"So..."

So the penny had dropped after all. Ashraf waited patiently, wanting Tom to spell it out before he brought the whole subject crashing to a halt again.

"You're...T?"

Ashraf wanted to crack a joke about Sustanon but resisted the urge. It would only fly over Tom's head anyway.

"You're trans?"

Ashraf put his hands in his pockets and nodded.

"Oh."

Tom was going very red and stopped short of the cafe doors to clear his throat and shuffle his feet.

"I just want to say, uh, that's, you know. Fine. By me. I mean, I'm okay with that. And if I should, er, I mean, if you have another, um, name you prefer or you want me to say they or she, then—"

Ashraf smirked.

"Other way around, mate."

Tom stopped mid-ramble, and his eyes nearly bugged out of his head.

"No way."

Ashraf shrugged.

"Holy *hell*."

"I appreciate the thought," Ashraf said as he opened the door, "but I don't really care if you approve or not. I don't identify as anything but a man anymore, and I have no intention of coming out now that I can pass for what I actually am. So thanks for the pep talk, but it's off limits and none of your business."

Tom huffed a short laugh.

"Okay. Yeah. I—guess so."

"We all right?"

"If I get a wedding invite."

Ashraf laughed and the door closed behind both of them.

"We're not planning anything until after Jamie graduates, so don't be a dick in the next couple of years, and you should be fine."

Chapter Twenty-Five

THE ROUTINE CHANGED again as spring burned bright and shifted into the beginnings of a scalding summer.

Wednesdays, they kept going swimming. Ashraf was beginning to genuinely enjoy puttering slowly up and down the pool in his slow lane, while Jamie created small tsunamis in the fast line every time they did a tumble turn. And going home afterwards on the train, damp and warm and Jamie shamelessly clinging to him like he was a support rail was an added bonus.

And on Saturday mornings, the beach.

Well—sort of.

Getting down onto the sand at low tide was actually surprisingly easy. The beach was deeper than the one in Aqaba, and the North Sea's noise as it bellowed and battered itself against the shore was, against all his logic insisting the opposite would be true, better for judging its reach. He got used to walking down the front in the shadow of the wall, barefoot in cool sand and eating ice cream with Jamie. When Ellie came down with the kids for a visit one weekend, he even managed to squat down in the sand with Sammy, halfway between water and wall, and help her build a sandcastle.

"You'd make a good dad, you know," Jamie said.

For the first time in his life, Ashraf wavered.

"Maybe we'll talk about that someday."

Jamie raised their eyebrows. "Seriously?"

"Yeah. Maybe. No promises."

Jamie laughed. "Well, I did agree to marry you on the assumption there'd be no babies—but if I get to have a baby, I'm not going to complain."

"Just bear in mind it wouldn't be mine. Never froze any eggs."

"Um, or mine! I didn't mean get pregnant, no *way*!"

They chose the wrong time to talk about it, as Sammy immediately demanded to know what eggs were and why Ashraf couldn't have babies, and it all got sidelined in favour of some seriously awkward—and terrible—excuses to not have to explain sex and gender to someone else's four-year-old.

The more they walked, and the more he stopped side-eyeing the brass bursting of the sea on the shore, the more Ashraf felt that dizzy fear easing its grip on his chest. The more he remembered the joy of the sea—the smell, the sound, the rough touch of sand under his bare toes and salt on his skin. The more part of him—a part he'd long since buried after the incident—wanted to roll up his jeans and wade out into the water with Jamie.

And slowly—over days and days and days—he began to inch down the sand towards the long foam fingers that crept in and out in ebbing waves. Slowly, he began to find flat stones for Jamie to skip, and waited for the water to rush out to step onto the cold, wet sand to hand them over. Slowly, he began to walk the edge of the water, rather than the edge of the wall, and yield to the allure of the sea.

He began to see things he'd not noticed—the ships on the horizon, the seals bobbing far out to sea, the birds swooping down on white-tipped waves to hunt—and things he'd forgotten, like the stranded jellyfish drying in the meagre British sun, and the deep prints of a child jumping in their father's bigger footsteps. He started to draw in the sand with his toes like a kid again, and wait to watch the sea wash it all away and offer up a clean slate, again and again and again.

"You really do love it, don't you?" Jamie asked one evening as they sat on the wall, brushing sand off their toes.

Ashraf, already de-sanded and re-shoed, shrugged. "I used to want to join the navy."

"Seriously?"

"Yeah. I mean, *used* to. I was a little kid back then."

"Still. Who knows. Maybe in another life, you'd have been the fish nerd, and I would have been into ancient history."

"I can't even persuade you into an archaeology trip."

"Not without a beach break."

"Tell you what," Ashraf said. "Find an ancient shipwreck or something, or some sunken Stone Age civilisation, and I'll sit on the boat watching your camera feed while you swim around it."

"Deal," Jamie said, laughing and standing up for a kiss. They drummed their fists on his chest, beaming. "Don't be so sceptical about diving with me one day, you know. It's only been six, seven months since you couldn't step onto the beach at Aqaba."

"Yeah..."

"Maybe you only had a minor phobia."

Ashraf raised his eyebrows. "I had nightmares at the sound of the sea."

"True. Okay, fine, maybe you're a stubborn shit."

"Maybe it's not me, it's you."

"Nope." A hand clapped over his mouth. "Nope! That way lies mush!"

Ashraf pulled his face free, seized Jamie in a bear hug, and twirled them before dropping them and kissing them sharply to stop any more protests.

"Rude," Jamie muttered against his mouth.

"Yeah, whatever."

"Want to get married on a beach?"

"If it meant I don't have to get married in a fish tank or a—"

"An aquarium!" Jamie's face lit up.

"Oh, *no*."

"An aquarium wedding, *yes*, that would be—"

"I take it back. I'm breaking up with you."

"No chance," Jamie said, throwing their arms around his neck with a laugh. They hung there deliberately, beaming, the wind ruffling up their hair and making them look doubly attractive, and doubly ridiculous.

"Divorced."

"Nope!" Their legs wound around his hips, as clever as their niece, and he laughed, staggered off down the seafront with Jamie hanging off him like a leech and crying for their fish tank wedding at the top of their lungs.

They must have both looked completely mad—and suddenly, he realised that Professor Ry—that *Alison*, was right.

Jamie was good for him, but it wasn't for making him brave or making him determined.

It was for lighting the fire under him that made him want to find those parts of himself, where he'd consigned them to his own history.

IT HAPPENED IN early July. A summer evening. Warm. The sun sinking slowly in the west, forever disappointingly not over the sea. The only sound, aside from the water, was a dog crashing into the foam after sticks, and a small child crying as it was wrestled into its mother's car to go home after a long day out on the sand. Peaceful. Tranquil. And after so many years, perhaps one of Ashraf's happier places once more.

Jamie was skipping stones, deliberately trying to get them to crash through the white foam as waves curled over and crashed onto the beach. The wind was picking up, plucking flecks off the crests and blurring the lines. The crash was loud, but the tide itself was quiet.

Ashraf swallowed.

They'd be going to Cairns in a week. Jamie would be out on the reef all day, every day. Well, almost every day. And Ashraf could swim in a pool, walk on the beach, stand and watch the elements rage, even enjoy them. But he still stopped short of the reach of the tide.

Jamie was standing ankle-deep in the waves, skipping the stones. When the water rushed back out, sand flowed through their toes and left half-buried feet behind. Then the next wave would crash over them and start it all over again. And Jamie stood through it all, over and over, immoveable and ignorant of how arrogantly powerful they looked just by doing so.

Ashraf could just step forward five paces and join them.

Just walk into the water, just up to his ankles, sling an arm over their shoulders, and skip stones with them. If he could do that, then he could get on the boat at Cairns. If he could get into the sea, just up to his ankles, then he could get on the boat.

Five paces.

Jamie turned to grin, throwing both hands up in a triumphant manner as a stone crashed through another otherwise perfect wave. They were beaming. Their hair was a mess from the wind. Their T-shirt rode up to show a slip of belly between jeans and cotton.

And Ashraf stepped forward.

He caught their hips in both hands and kissed them sharply, just as the cold water rushed over his feet. The sand slid out from under him. Jamie laughed into his mouth, their arms coming up around his neck.

And he laughed back, giddy with fear and exhilaration. The sea. The *sea*. He was standing in the sea. He'd done it, after all this time; he'd finally gone and *done* it.

Thanks to the person clutching tight to his neck, hanging off him like he was their world.

The person who'd screamed and said yes.

The person he was going to marry.

But not in an aquarium.

"Love you," Jamie whispered, stretching up on their toes despite the sliding sand. They drummed their fists on Ashraf's chest as another wave rolled in, and Ashraf's heart hammered in time with them.

"Reckon I'm ready for Australia?"

"Fuck Australia," Jamie said and grinned. "Reckon you're ready for *me*?"

Chapter Twenty-Six

DUSK WAS FALLING when the plane wheels squealed on the runway. Ashraf had forced himself to stare at the shimmering sea as they'd come down, but it was swallowed by the land and disappeared when they touched down. And he found himself staring, instead, at a small airport under a gold-streaked sky.

Cairns.

They'd set off a full thirty hours earlier, and it was more than a little bit of a mindfuck to be staring at dusk. The layover in Singapore had been enough to handle, and Ashraf had wanted to take up drinking for the first time in his life just to manage the fact that his brain felt like it had been fried after so long in recycled air and cramped space. Only then, they'd boarded another flight, and now here they were.

In Cairns.

In Australia. And out there, under that shimmering gold sea, was the reef everyone but Ashraf had come so far to see.

Professor Hanley was triply haphazard in an airport, it turned out, with poor George in charge of his passport and papers like they were an old married couple instead of a mad professor and his long-suffering assistant. Meg was half-asleep, and Jamie was grumpy, fit to be tied when Ashraf's dark skin and faint accent earned him a long, awkward moment at border control.

It was night before they got out and found George's hire car. Professor Hanley rumbled that he was perfectly capable of driving, and then started snoring in the passenger seat the moment they peeled out of the parking area. Jamie dozed against Ashraf's shoulder, as they had been doing for most of the last leg of the journey. Ashraf stared out into the dark, and couldn't see the sea.

There was a knot in his chest. They'd be going to sea tomorrow.

Or rather, Jamie would. They'd said Ashraf could stay on land the whole time if he wanted. And Ashraf *did* want—but he also wanted to see Jamie lit up and excited about their fish. He wanted to see Jamie at their most beautiful, where they felt most at home. He wanted to overcome the last hurdle. He wanted to be as powerful as Jamie had looked in the North Sea, as immortal as he'd felt when he'd waded out to kiss them in the surf at sunset. He wanted to go out to sea with his partner, wanted to take his fear and kiss it between the eyes, and never be afraid again.

And he was terrified.

Thankfully, the apartments were several streets inland. He couldn't hear the water, even in the quiet night, and the stack of brochures in the lobby reminded him what else Cairns had to offer. If he couldn't do it, he could always go and see the rainforest and the waterfalls. Jamie would like those too, so they could take a couple of days out together. And he had his paper to be working on anyway, a whole hard drive of research to be getting on with. Logically, there was no harm in not managing it. Logically, there was nothing to lose.

Jamie loved him. And love didn't care if he could get on the boat or not.

He could cross tomorrow's bridge...tomorrow.

"I'm knackered," Jamie grumbled as they headed upstairs to their apartment, after fending off the professor's attempts at a group drink at the bar on the ground floor. "I want to sleep for a thousand years."

"Well, you didn't sleep on either of the flights," Ashraf pointed out.

"Hate long-haul flights," came the complaint. "Why is Australia so far away?"

Ashraf shrugged as he unlocked the door, and Jamie sighed in relief when they saw the bed. King-size, and with a daft number of pillows. The apartment was small—little more than a kitchenette, a bedroom through an archway, and a bathroom kitted out like a wet room—but it would do. The most important part, right now, was the mattress. Jamie stripped without a second thought and crawled up onto the sheets to collapse right in the middle.

"Don't you want a shower first?" Ashraf asked.

A soft snore was his only reply, and he chuckled. He dropped their bags and rummaged for a pair of boxers. The odds of Jamie getting horny in the night were pretty low if they were that tired, but it had become a tradition now, and Jamie never minded. When he found a suitable pair, he stepped over to the bed and gently slid them over Jamie's feet and up their legs. All he got, when he snapped the waistband into place, was a sleepy mumble and a vague swat in his direction.

"Love you too, sweetheart," he said when he recognised the profanity, and smirked when he earned himself a snort.

He carefully folded the duvet over to cocoon Jamie in a burrito, deciding to get them under the sheets when he settled down for the night. For now, he had to shower. The staleness of recycled air was clinging to him, and his eyes felt dry and gritty. It was also morning back home, and his body knew it. Shower, prayers to reset his routine, and then bed.

And tomorrow...tomorrow he could face the music.

Or the water.

ASHRAF WAS WOKEN by lips on his eyelids. He hummed, nudging his face into the kisses, stretched as his beard was rubbed by a clean jaw like an affectionate cat was sharing his sheets, and then relaxed and looped an arm blindly around slim hips when a mouth touched his own, and opened him up to be appreciated.

"S'the time?" he mumbled when he was able, and a little laugh reached his ears.

"Don't care. Early. C'mere."

They wound around each other in the darkness under the duvet. Jamie curled up in Ashraf's arms, tucked against his chest and rubbing their face into his skin. If they could purr, Ashraf imagined they would. He closed his eyes, nose buried in their fine hair, and stroked miles of smooth skin. From the long valley of a sleek spine to the soft swell above their thighs, and around to the gentle, enticing jut of hips before tracing the backs of his fingernails up over the soft pulse hidden in their chest and neck and finishing on their delicate earlobes—only, once there, to begin all over again.

Eventually, though, Jamie's want for a good cuddle seemed to give way to what always happened if Ashraf paid too much attention to that little soft spot just above the lip of their hip, where bone met belly, and they crept away after one last kiss to shower and, most likely, take care of some other needs. Ashraf left them to it, stretching luxuriously in the messy sheets before getting out of bed and peering cautiously out of the window.

Something shimmered beyond the trees.

The sea.

He still couldn't hear it, over the traffic in the road below and a couple of men arguing loudly in the street about someone called Jenna. But he knew it was there.

He rubbed his fingers over his neck, where Jamie had kissed him, and squared his shoulders. He could do this. He'd done braver, madder, more dangerous things than get on a boat and paddle out to sea. And he could swim. Jamie had promised a lifejacket. And Ashraf wasn't going underwater.

He wasn't going underwater.

He held onto the thought as they both got ready, Jamie still in a cosy mood. It took twice as long as usual, through all the kisses and the fact they'd sit on Ashraf's lap every time he sat down. They stuffed their bikini tops into their bag and laughed at Ashraf's expression.

"I have a feeling you're going to try coming out with us to the site, but you might need a little bit of hand-holding. And as much fun as earning some dirty looks are, I don't think it'll help today."

Ashraf grimaced. "That doesn't mean you have to—"

"It's *fine*," Jamie said, rising into a point to kiss his cheek. "Trust me. And it's warm enough I'll appreciate the lack of clothes."

"Surprised you're not going topless, then," he said, attempting a joke.

"George complains," Jamie said, rolling their eyes. "You going to come out to sea?"

"I—hope so?"

"We're not diving today. Any of us. We're going out to drop some cameras and get some footage. They want us to select a spot and get the framework down on this trip."

"So why not dive? Isn't that faster?"

"Can't dive right after a flight," Jamie said cheerily as Ashraf shut the apartment door behind the pair of them. "The pressure changes can make you really ill. Meg and I are going to dive tomorrow. The professor can't dive at all since his surgery—that's why he brings two hapless idiots. I mean, students."

Ashraf rolled his eyes.

"Hey, you do the same for digs."

"I don't *go* to digs."

"Exactly!"

"And I don't have students to send anyway."

"You will, budding professor."

Ashraf rolled his eyes again, so hard they ached, and Jamie laughed at him and called him melodramatic.

It was an easy start to the morning. They met some Australian researchers in a cafe and talked for a good couple of hours about fish and other things Ashraf had no interest in. He sat back, nursed a coffee, and got through a couple of papers that Tom had sent him—rumblings of some new research possibilities about early man's religious understandings via common colour usage across numerous sites. Although, personally, Ashraf thought colour availability would be the major roadblock there.

It was half eleven before the chattering died off into something approaching consensus, and then the group began to gather their bags and get up again. The Australians left one by one until only a woman around Professor Hanley's age remained, and they gushed about crayfish all the way out onto the esplanade.

The sea murmured.

The knot from last night formed in Ashraf's chest again. They were heading to a pier or marina. Boats were bobbing on the surface of the water. He could see seaweed. A bottle. Debris, just drifting by, like—

"Hey."

Jamie's fingers were warm on his wrist. Ashraf wriggled his arm until their fingers could slide between his own.

"I'm okay."

"You don't look it."

"Thanks."

Jamie stopped. George glanced back over his shoulder, mouth open to call them, then hesitated and turned away again. Ashraf swallowed, grateful for the illusion of privacy.

"You don't have to do this."

"I know."

He did. But if he didn't—then what? When would he finally do it? And if he never did...

How long before he simply missed too much of Jamie's passions to keep hold of them?

"If you're not ready," Jamie said gently, "then that's fine. I mean—we can't turn back, Ash. Once we launch, we're launched. We won't be able to come back to shore if you're having a panic attack. Maybe it would be better to try it out at the weekend, just us, just hire a speedboat or something and—"

"No."

Jamie blinked and fell silent.

"If I'm ever going to get past this," Ashraf muttered, "then I need to—to just do it."

"Cue the advert," Jamie quipped.

"I can swim. I can stand in the sea with you. This—this is fine. I can do this. I *need* to do this."

Jamie cocked their head.

"Do you need to do this for me," they said, "or for you?"

Ashraf stared.

Then cupped their face in both hands and kissed them.

It was chaste and sweet. Innocent. Their fingers curled around his wrists, but they pushed up on their toes to be closer. They held him at bay and pulled him closer all at once, and he poured everything he could possibly feel into that simple, trusting, gentle kiss.

"I don't need to do this for you," he whispered. "You love me. We shouldn't even work, and individually, we're both pretty damn impressive."

Jamie chuckled.

"But together? Together, we're incredible. We're beyond belief when we're together. And if I'm part of something—this thing—that's so completely brilliant in every way, then where does the sea get off thinking I'm going to be afraid of a little boat?"

Jamie laughed.

"Technically, that doesn't answer my question."

"For me," Ashraf said clearly. "I'm done being afraid. Of anything. Including that."

"Good," Jamie said and swiped their nose against his before backing off. "In any case, there's no reason to be afraid anyway, even if you weren't a superhero. There's lifejackets. You can wear one all afternoon if you want. And we can sort you a safety line."

"Don't think I'm going anywhere near the railing."

"I, um...given what happened, I'd recommend you stay on deck."

Ashraf hesitated. "Why?"

"The boat's got a viewing window."

"A what?"

"A glass bottom."

The way the water had rubbed itself against the car windows burst into Ashraf's mind, and he shivered.

"Right."

"You don't have to."

"I know. I'm going to."

Jamie tugged lightly. "C'mon, then. Tell you what. If you get on board and come out with us, I'll let you pick the colour."

"What—"

There it was.

It was just a little boat. Ashraf didn't know anything about boats, but even he knew this one was little. Small, white, big sail, motor on the back. Little cabin with a wheel. Small deck all the way around, ending in a point at the front. It didn't look big enough for ten people, but that's how many—including them—had gathered on the boards. It was moored with heavy, damp ropes, and the water licked its hull in wet slaps.

And the hull sat high. Bobbing. Floating.

Suddenly, all his bravado felt thin.

"C'mon," Jamie said softly and stepped up onto the side. It was only a foot from the pier. It rose and fell gently as Ashraf stared. "Babe? C'mon."

Jamie's hand was held out towards him.

He could go back. He could.

The water had closed over the roof of the car with that same terrible slapping sound...

He couldn't go back.

Ashraf took a deep breath—and gripped Jamie's hand. Stepped up on shaky legs. Steadied himself against the cabin wall as the world rocked underneath him, and he left the land behind. And then Jamie was crowding him into that wall, arms around his neck and lips at his ear. Warm. Wonderful.

Powerful.

"You get to pick the colour now."

"W-what colour?" Ashraf mumbled weakly, wanting to hug back but not wanting to let go of the side.

"My bikini top."

People were shouting. The world was swaying. He could hear Professor Hanley bleating in the background, something about motor noise, and George's answering grumble. The boat was moving.

Ashraf screwed up his face and opened his eyes. To see water. Sea. Filling a growing gulf between the ship and the shore. The pier was drifting away. They were going out to sea. Leaving the land behind, and going out to see all of the life underwater.

For the first time in twenty-six years, he was at sea.

"Hey," Jamie whispered, right there at his front. "You want to see a secret?"

"A secret?" he croaked.

"Mhmm. I was going to show you tonight, but I think you earned it now."

"What's tha—"

They tugged the very edge of their shorts down. And in the tiny gap between their hip bone and the first strands of dark pubic hair, lay a word. In his own handwriting. In Arabic.

Fish.

Ashraf touched the very tip of his finger to it and smiled.

"Blue."

"Blue?"

"Your bikini top. I pick blue."

Jamie cocked their head. "I thought you liked me in red best?"

"I do," he said. "But here we are. Here *I* am."

At sea.

So he chose blue, in honour of the occasion.

About the Author

Matthew J. Metzger is an ace, trans author posing as a functional human being in the wilds of Yorkshire, England. Although mainly a writer of contemporary, working-class romance, he also strays into fantasy when the mood strikes. Whatever the genre, the focus is inevitably on queer characters and their relationships, be they familial, platonic, sexual, or romantic.

When not crunching numbers at his day job, or writing books by night, Matthew can be found tweeting from the gym, being used as a pillow by his cat, or trying to keep his website in some semblance of order.

Email: mattmetzger@hotmail.co.uk

Facebook: www.facebook.com/mattjmetzger

Twitter: www.twitter.com/MatthewJMetzger

Website: www.matthewjmetzger.com

Other books by this author

Walking on Water
Big Man

Coming Soon from Matthew J. Metzger

Bump

David's pregnant.

He's always wanted to have children, and being a stepfather for the past two years has been a great adventure. There'd even been a plan to start looking into adoption and turn their family of three into four.

But now there's a bump, and David doesn't know what to do. He's spent years escaping the grip of his own body and burying the past—but there's no way he can hide from his history if he lets the bump get any bigger. It's not just his baby; it's also his breakdown.

He doesn't know if he can do this.

Also Available from NineStar Press

Connect with NineStar Press

Website: NineStarPress.com

Facebook: NineStarPress

Facebook Reader Group: NineStarNiche

Twitter: @ninestarpress

Tumblr: NineStarPress

www.ingramcontent.com/pod-product-compliance
Lightning Source LLC
Chambersburg PA
CBHW060541190726
48283CB00003B/819